I0788533

Navigating the Path to College

A Comprehensive Guide for High School Students and Parents,

Specifically, for immigrant parents

BY

Solomon Sahle

COLLEGE

Background

Greetings to the readers,

I am Solomon Sahle, and it is with great pleasure that I share with you a glimpse into my journey and the inspiration behind this guide for high school students, seeking the path to college. With a deep-rooted passion for education and a commitment to empowering young minds, I have spent the last 15 years immersed in the world of mentoring and tutoring high school students.

My story begins with a profound belief in the transformative power of education. Having witnessed the transformative impact that guidance can have on a student's academic and personal journey, I dedicated myself to becoming a mentor and guide for those navigating the critical juncture between high school and college. Over the years, I have had the privilege of engaging with countless students, understanding their aspirations, fears, and the challenges they face in pursuing higher education.

This book, born out of years of hands-on experience and enriched by conversations with students and their parents, is a reflection of the collective wisdom garnered from these interactions. It is not only a compilation of strategies but a testament to the belief that every student deserves access to the guidance necessarily to unlock their full potential.

Crafting Guidance for the College Journey

Within the pages of this book, you will find a tapestry woven from my experiences, conversations, and a voracious appetite for knowledge from various academic resources. The journey of crafting this guide involved countless hours of listening, learning, and distilling insights to provide a comprehensive resource for high school students aiming for higher education.

Navigating the labyrinth of college applications, standardized tests, and the myriad of choices can be overwhelming. My goal is to demystify this process and offer a roadmap that not only informs but empowers students to make informed decisions about their future. This guide covers everything from choosing the right courses and extracurricular activities to tackling the daunting college application essays.

As an author, mentor, and advocate for education, I invite you to join me on this expedition, where the destination is not just admission to college but the cultivation of a mindset that embraces lifelong learning and personal growth. The experiences shared in these pages are not just mine; they are the stories of the resilient students I've had the privilege of guiding.

May this guide serve as a compass, lighting the way for high school students as they embark on their unique journey towards higher education. Here's to unlocking the doors of opportunity and fostering a generation of empowered, confident, and informed individuals ready to navigate the world of academia.

Contents

Chapter 1
Introduction

The significance of a college education in today's world

In today's rapidly evolving world, a college education holds immense significance for high school students in the United States. Gone are the days, when a high school diploma would guarantee steady employment and a promising future. As the job market becomes increasingly competitive, employers are placing greater emphasis on higher education qualifications.

A college education offers numerous advantages and opportunities that can shape a student's life in profound ways. Firstly, obtaining a degree greatly enhances one's knowledge and skills in a specific field of study. Whether it's engineering, business, arts, or sciences, a college education provides students with a comprehensive understanding and specialized expertise that can open doors to exciting career prospects.

Beyond the acquisition of knowledge, college is a transformative experience that promotes personal growth and development. It exposes students to a diverse range of ideas, cultures, and perspectives, fostering critical thinking, intellectual curiosity, and empathy. The college environment encourages students to step out of their comfort zones, engage in stimulating discussions, and challenge their preconceived notions. These experiences cultivate lifelong skills such as effective communication, teamwork, and adaptability, which are highly valued by employers in today's globalized economy.

Moreover, a college degree significantly impacts earning potential. Studies consistently show that individuals with a bachelor's degree earn higher salaries and experience greater job security compared to those without a degree. In fact, the wage gap between college graduates and high school graduates has been steadily widening over the years. By investing in a college education, students greatly increase their chances of securing a financially stable future and enjoying a higher standard of living.

In addition to the individual benefits, a college education also brings about positive societal and community impacts. College graduates often contribute to the advancement of society through innovation, research, and social entrepreneurship. They are more likely to be engaged citizens, voting in elections, volunteering, and actively participating in community initiatives. By obtaining a college education, students are better equipped to make meaningful contributions to their communities and contribute to the overall progress of society.

As we embark on this journey together, it is crucial to recognize the significance of a college education and the opportunities it can unlock. Throughout this guide, we will provide you with valuable insights and practical strategies to navigate the college application process successfully. So, let us begin this transformative adventure and set realistic goals and expectations, as we embark on the path to securing a place in a good college or university

Goal setting for college applications

A college education is becoming increasingly crucial for high school students in the United States. As the job market becomes more competitive, a college degree provides knowledge and specialized skills in a specific field, promotes personal growth, and develops critical thinking and communication skills. It also significantly impacts earning potential and contributes to societal and community advancement.

Welcome to "A Guide for USA High School Students to Get to College." In this book, we will provide you with expert insights, practical strategies, and real-world data analysis to help you navigate the college application process successfully.

In this chapter, we will set the stage for your college journey, emphasizing the importance of a college education and helping you set realistic goals and expectations. We understand that this can be an overwhelming time for both students and parents, so we aim to provide you with a comprehensive overview of the college application process and its significance in a student's life.

The college application process involves several steps, from researching colleges and universities to submitting applications and securing financial aid. Our goal is to equip you with the knowledge and tools necessary to make informed decisions and tackle each step of the process with confidence.

Throughout the book, we will adhere to certain guidelines to ensure the information we provide is relevant, accurate, and valuable to all readers. We will avoid focusing on overly specific details about individual institutions, as these can vary frequently and may not be useful in a general guide. We will also refrain from giving specific legal or financial advice, as these will depend on individual circumstances and require professional advice.

Our approach will be objective and informative, maintaining a didactic and educational tone. We will avoid personal opinions or bias toward particular institutions or educational paths, allowing you to make your own informed choices.

While we strive to provide accurate and up-to-date information, it's important to note that procedures and admission requirements can change over time. Therefore, we encourage you to double-check any specific information against official college websites or consult with your school's college counselor.

Throughout each chapter, we will include expert insights, practical strategies, and real-world examples to enhance your understanding and provide you with actionable steps to achieve your college goals.

Are you ready to embark on this exciting journey towards college? Let's dive into the world of college applications and discover the path to your future success.

Expectations vs. Reality in the College Application Journey

Setting realistic goals and expectations is crucial when embarking on the college application journey. Many students have grand visions of their dream college, envisioning a seamless and effortless path to acceptance. However, it is important to acknowledge that the reality of the college application process can be quite different from these expectations.

One common misconception among high school students is that getting into a top-tier college or university guarantees success in the future. While attending a prestigious institution can certainly open doors; it is not the sole determining factor of one's success. The journey to college involves various factors such as grades, extracurricular activities, essays, and standardized test scores, all of which play a role in the admissions process.

Another expectation students often have is that there is one "perfect" college for them, and any other options are considered as a failure. This mindset can lead to unnecessary stress and disappointment. It is essential to recognize that there are many excellent colleges and universities across the United States, each offering unique academic programs and opportunities. The key is to find the college that aligns with the student's interests, goals, and values rather than solely focusing on name recognition.

Furthermore, the college application process is not always as straightforward as students may initially believe. There are numerous deadlines to meet, essays to write, recommendations to gather, and financial aid applications to submit. It can be overwhelming, and unexpected challenges may arise along the way. Understanding and preparing for these challenges will help students navigate the process more effectively.

Throughout this book, we will not only provide expert insights and practical strategies but also address the realities of the college application journey. We will encourage students and parents to have clear expectations, emphasizing that success is not solely defined by attending a certain college or university. Our aim is to empower students to make informed decisions, leverage their strengths, and embrace the opportunities available to them.

To ensure the most accurate and up-to-date information, we recommend that readers verify specific details with official college websites or college counselors. Additionally, we will provide real-world examples and stories to illustrate the various aspects of the college application process, allowing students to gain insights from those who have successfully navigated the journey.

As we embark on this journey together, let us embrace the reality of the college application process, acknowledging the challenges and celebrating the achievements. By setting realistic goals and expectations, students can confidently navigate the path towards their desired college, equipped with the knowledge and strategies provided in this guide.

An overview of the college application process

The college application process can often seem overwhelming, but with careful planning and preparation, it can also be an exciting opportunity for growth and self-discovery. This chapter will provide you with an overview of the important steps involved in applying to college, allowing you to approach the process with confidence and a clear understanding of what to expect.

First and foremost, it's crucial to understand that college applications are highly competitive. This means that you will need to put in the effort to stand out from the crowd. However, it's also important to keep in mind that attending a top-tier college does not guarantee success. Instead, it's essential to find a college that aligns with your interests, values, and goals.

The college application journey begins with researching colleges and universities that meet your criteria. Consider factors such as location, size, majors and programs offered, commute, campus culture, and extracurricular opportunities. While there are numerous college-ranking lists available, they should be used as a starting point rather than the sole determinant of your choices.

Once you have identified potential colleges, it's important to understand their admission requirements. This includes understanding the necessary standardized tests, such as the

SAT or ACT, and their respective deadlines. Additionally, you should familiarize yourself with the specific application materials required by each institution, such as essays, recommendation letters, and transcripts.

It is highly recommended to create a timeline for completing all the necessary tasks. This will help you stay organized and ensure that you don't miss any deadlines. Keep in mind that some colleges have early admission programs with earlier deadlines, so planning ahead will give you an advantage.

While collecting personal documents and academic records, make sure to maintain accurate and up-to-date records. It's also prudent to obtain multiple copies of important documents to avoid any last-minute complications.

As you begin writing your college essays, remember that they provide an opportunity for admissions officers to get to know you beyond your academic achievements. Be genuine and authentic in your writing, sharing personal stories or experiences that highlight your strengths and values. Utilize the feedback from trusted mentors, teachers, or counselors to help polish your essays and make them stand out.

In addition to essays, letters of recommendation serve as valuable insights into your character and abilities. Reach out to teachers, coaches, or community leaders who know you well and can speak to your strengths. Building strong relationships with your recommenders and providing them with ample time and information will greatly benefit your application.

Lastly, but crucially, be prepared to tackle financial aid and scholarship applications. College can be expensive, but there are various financial aid options available to help make it more affordable. Be sure to research and understand the different types of financial aid, such as grants, scholarships, loans, and work-study programs. Keep track of application deadlines for financial aid, as they may differ from regular admissions deadlines.

Remember, that the college application process is a journey, not just a means to an end. Embrace the opportunity to learn more about yourself, explore new possibilities, and grow as an individual. By staying organized, proactive, and true to yourself, you can navigate the college application process successfully and open doors to a bright future. Good luck on your journey!

Chapter 2
Understanding College Options

Exploring Different Types of Colleges

When it comes to choosing a college, there are several types of institutions to consider. Understanding the differences between these options is crucial in making an informed decision about your educational path. Let's explore some of the common types of colleges available to high school students.

1. Community Colleges:

Community colleges, also known as junior colleges, offer two-year associate degree programs as well as vocational and technical training programs. These institutions are often affordable and provide a supportive environment for students who wish to explore different career options or transfer to a four-year college later on.

2. Liberal Arts Colleges:

Liberal arts colleges emphasize a well-rounded education, focusing on humanities, sciences, and social sciences. They offer bachelor's degrees and are known for providing small class sizes, highly engaged faculty, and a strong emphasis on critical thinking and analytical skills. Liberal arts colleges are a great choice for students who value personalized attention and a broad-based education.

3. Research Universities:

Research universities are larger institutions that offer a wide range of academic programs, including undergraduate, graduate, and professional degrees. These universities often have extensive research facilities and faculty conducting cutting-edge research. They provide opportunities for students to engage in research projects, internships, and collaborations with renowned experts.

4. Public Institutions:

Public colleges and universities are funded by state governments and often offer more affordable tuition rates for in-state students. These institutions can range in size, academic offerings, and campus culture. Public universities are known for their diverse student populations and typically offer a broad array of programs and resources.

5. Private Institutions:

Private colleges and universities are funded through tuition and private donations. They often have higher tuition fees compared to public institutions but may also have more financial aid options available. Private institutions can vary in size, focus, and academic offerings, and they often provide a close-knit community and smaller class sizes.

6. Trade Schools and Vocational Education:

Trade schools and vocational education programs focus on specific trades or professions, such as nursing, automotive technology, culinary arts, or graphic design. These programs offer hands-on training and prepare students for direct entry into the workforce. Trade schools can be a great option for students who have a clear career path in mind and want to gain practical skills quickly.

Understanding the different types of colleges will help you narrow down your options and find the institutions that align with your educational goals and personal preferences. In the next chapter, we will explore how to research and evaluate colleges to determine which ones are the best fit for you.

Comparing public and private institutions

When considering college options, it's important to understand the differences between public and private institutions. While both types of colleges offer valuable educational opportunities, there are distinct characteristics that can impact your college experience.

One of the main differences between public and private institutions is their funding. Public colleges are primarily funded by state governments, which often results in lower tuition fees for in-state students. Private colleges, on the other hand, rely on tuition and private donations to support their operations, making them generally more expensive.

Class size is another factor to consider. Public colleges tend to have larger class sizes, which can result in less individualized attention from professors. Private colleges, on the other hand, often have smaller class sizes, allowing for more personalized interactions and a closer-knit community.

The curriculum and academic programs can also differ between public and private institutions. Public colleges often have a wider range of majors and program offerings due to their larger size and resources. Private colleges may focus on specific areas of study, such as liberal arts or specialized professional fields.

Campus culture is another aspect that can vary between public and private institutions. Public colleges tend to have a more diverse student body and offer a wide range of extracurricular activities and organizations. Private colleges often emphasize a sense of community and may have a more tight-knit campus life.

Another consideration is the admissions process. Public colleges often have larger applicant pools, which can make the admissions process more competitive. Private colleges may have more holistic admissions criteria and take into account factors beyond just grades and test scores.

Ultimately, choosing between a public or private institution depends on your individual preferences and goals. Public colleges may offer more affordability and variety, while private colleges may provide a more intimate learning environment and specialized programs. It's important to research and visit different colleges to get a feel for their campus culture and academic offerings before making a decision. In the following chapters, we will explore additional factors to consider and guide you through the college selection process.

The role of community colleges.

Community colleges play a vital role in the educational landscape, offering students a more affordable and flexible pathway to higher education. These institutions, often referred to as junior colleges or two-year colleges, are typically public institutions; that provide a wide range of associate degree programs, vocational training, and certificate courses.

One of the main advantages of attending a community college is the lower cost of tuition compared to four-year colleges and universities. This affordability factor makes it an attractive option for students who want to save money or are unsure of their long-term educational goals. By starting at a community college, students can significantly reduce the financial burden of obtaining a degree.

In addition to cost savings, community colleges offer greater flexibility in terms of scheduling and enrollment. Many students choose to attend community colleges while working part-time or juggling family responsibilities. These colleges often have evening and weekend classes, making it easier for individuals with busy schedules to pursue higher education.

Furthermore, community colleges provide a supportive learning environment for students who may need additional academic assistance. They offer resources such as tutoring services, writing centers, and study groups to help students succeed academically. This support is particularly beneficial for students who may have struggled in high school or need to improve their academic skills before transitioning to a four-year institution.

Another advantage of attending a community college is the opportunity to explore different academic and career paths. Community colleges offer a wide range of programs and majors, allowing students to sample various fields of study before committing to a specific career track. This can save students from spending time and money pursuing a degree that they later realize may not align with their interests or goals.

Furthermore, community colleges often have articulation agreements with four-year colleges and universities. These agreements facilitate the seamless transfer of credits earned at the community college to the four-year institution. By starting at a community college and transferring to a four-year institution, students can save money on tuition while still obtaining a bachelor's degree from a reputable university.

It is important to note that while community colleges provide a solid foundation for higher education, they may have certain limitations. Some career paths, such as those in highly specialized fields like medicine or engineering, may require students to transfer to a four-year institution, after completing their general education requirements at a community college.

In conclusion, community colleges offer an affordable and flexible pathway to higher education for students. They provide a supportive environment, a variety of academic programs, and the opportunity to explore different career paths. However, it is crucial for students to research and understand the limitations of community colleges in relation to their specific educational and career goals.

Understanding trade schools and vocational education

Trade schools and vocational education offer alternative paths for students who are interested in pursuing career-specific training and acquiring practical skills. While traditional colleges and universities focus on providing a broad-based education, trade schools and vocational programs concentrate on specific trades and industries.

Trade schools, also known as technical schools or career colleges, offer specialized training in fields such as automotive technology, culinary arts, cosmetology, plumbing, electrical work, and many others. These programs typically range from a few months to two years in duration. Unlike traditional colleges, trade schools prioritize hands-on learning and practical experience in their curriculum.

One of the advantages of trade schools is their emphasis on preparing students for immediate entry into the job market. The skills obtained through trade school programs are often in high demand, making graduates more employable. Additionally, trade school education tends to be more cost-effective than a traditional four-year college degree.

Vocational education is a broader term that encompasses trade schools but also includes programs offered in high schools and community colleges. These programs prepare students for specific occupations and provide a blend of academic and technical training. Vocational education programs are designed to equip students with skills that are directly applicable to various industries, such as healthcare, information technology, construction, and manufacturing.

One notable advantage of vocational education is the opportunity for students to gain industry certifications while still in school. These certifications can greatly enhance a student's employability and may even lead to higher-paying jobs upon graduation. Vocational education programs also provide a pathway for students to continue their education at the college level, if they choose to pursue a more advanced degree in their chosen field.

It is important for students to carefully research and consider trade schools and vocational education programs before making a decision. Factors such as program accreditation, job placement rates, and the reputation of the institution should all be taken into account. Furthermore, students should evaluate their own career aspirations and interests to ensure that a trade school or vocational program aligns with their long-term goals.

In summary, trade schools and vocational education offer a viable alternative to traditional colleges and universities for students who prefer a more focused and hands-on approach to learning. These programs provide valuable skills and certifications that can lead to immediate employment opportunities in various industries. Students should thoroughly research and evaluate their options to determine if trade school or vocational education is the right path for them.

Chapter 3
Preparing Academically

Strategic selection of high school courses

Strategic selection of high school courses plays a crucial role in preparing academically for college. As you embark on your journey towards higher education, it's essential to choose your courses strategically to meet college admission requirements and align with your academic and career goals.

When selecting high school courses, start by reviewing the admission requirements of the colleges and universities you are interested in. College websites and admission guides provide detailed information on the recommended course load, including the number of years required in each subject area. Take note of any specific prerequisites or recommended courses for your intended major.

While it's important to meet the minimum requirements, don't limit yourself to just the basics. Challenge yourself by taking advanced or honors courses if they are available at your school. These courses not only demonstrate your academic rigor but also help you develop the skills necessary for success in college.

Consider taking a variety of courses across different subjects to gain a well-rounded education. Math, science, English, social studies, and foreign languages are typically expected subjects in most college applications. However, don't forget about other subjects like art, music, or computer science if they align with your interests or future career aspirations.

Additionally, explore opportunities for Advanced Placement (AP) or International Baccalaureate (IB) courses. These rigorous programs offer college-level coursework and provide the opportunity to earn college credit or advanced placement in college courses. However, be mindful of your own capabilities and workload. Taking on too much in these programs may lead to burnout and negatively impact your academic performance.

Beyond choosing the right courses, maintaining a strong GPA is crucial for college admission. Colleges and universities often consider your cumulative GPA as an indicator of your academic abilities and determination. Strive to earn good grades in all your courses and seek help if you're struggling in any subject.

While academics are essential, extracurricular activities also play a vital role in the college application process. Participating in extracurriculars demonstrates your leadership, teamwork, and time management skills. Consider joining clubs, sports teams, or community organizations that align with your interests and passions. These activities not only enhance your college application but also provide valuable experiences and personal growth.

As you choose your high school courses, strike a balance between academic rigor, your personal interests, and your capacity to excel. It's better to excel in a well-rounded set of courses rather than struggle with an overwhelming workload. Remember, the goal is not just to meet college admission requirements but also to prepare yourself for the academic challenges and opportunities that lie ahead.

In the next segment, we will dive deeper into the importance of maintaining a strong GPA and ways you can enhance your academic performance in preparation for college.

The importance of maintaining a strong GPA

Maintaining a strong GPA is crucial for high school students aiming to get into good colleges and universities. Your grade point average reflects your academic performance and is one of the key factors considered by admissions officers.

But why is GPA so important? Well, colleges want to admit students who demonstrate a consistent dedication to their studies and who can handle the rigor of college-level coursework. Your GPA serves as a measure of your ability to excel academically and meet the demands of higher education.

As you progress through high school, it's essential to prioritize your studies and strive for excellent grades. This doesn't mean you have to be a straight-A student in every subject, but you should aim for a GPA that reflects your best effort. Remember, colleges also consider the difficulty of your course load, so taking advanced or honors classes can help boost your GPA while challenging yourself intellectually.

In addition to demonstrating your academic abilities, a strong GPA also opens doors to scholarships, grants, and other financial aid opportunities. Many universities offer merit-based scholarships that reward students with high

GPAs, helping to alleviate the financial burden of college tuition.

To maintain a strong GPA, start by staying organized and managing your time effectively. Create a study schedule that allows you to dedicate sufficient time to each subject and complete assignments on time. Seek help from teachers or tutors if you're struggling with particular concepts or subjects.

It's also important to adopt good study habits, such as breaking larger tasks into smaller, manageable chunks, using effective note-taking techniques, and practicing regular review sessions. Don't cram for exams at the last minute; instead, develop a consistent study routine that promotes long-term retention of information.

Furthermore, make use of the resources available to you, such as libraries, online research databases, and study groups. Collaborating with classmates can not only enhance your understanding of the material but also expose you to different perspectives and approaches.

Remember, maintaining a strong GPA requires discipline and commitment. Avoid the temptation to procrastinate or slack off, as every grade counts towards your overall average. Take advantage of the opportunities provided by your high school to excel academically and set yourself up for success in the college admissions process.

In the next section, we will explore the impact of extracurricular activities on your college application and how to choose the right activities that align with your interests and goals.

Extracurricular activities and their role in college admissions

Extracurricular activities play a vital role in college admissions. While maintaining a strong GPA is crucial, colleges also look for well-rounded students who have engaged in activities outside of the classroom. These activities can showcase an individual's passions, talents, leadership skills, and ability to balance multiple commitments.

Participating in extracurricular activities demonstrates a student's dedication and willingness to go above and beyond their academic responsibilities. Colleges understand that not all learning happens within the confines of a classroom. They value students who have actively pursued their interests and made a positive impact in their communities.

When selecting extracurricular activities, it's important for students to choose those that align with their interests and strengths. Pursuing activities, they are passionate about not only allows them to enjoy their time outside of class but also helps them develop important skills and qualities that will benefit them in college and beyond.

Colleges appreciate students who have demonstrated leadership potential. Taking on leadership roles in clubs, sports teams, or community organizations shows initiative and the ability to inspire and influence others. Leadership experience can set a student apart from their peers, and show colleges that they have the potential to make a meaningful impact on campus.

It's also important for students to consider the quality of their involvement in extracurricular activities rather than the quantity. Admission officers value depth and consistency rather than a long list of superficial involvements. Students should aim to make a significant contribution to a few activities rather than spreading themselves too thin across many.

Extracurricular activities can also provide opportunities for students to develop important life skills such as teamwork, time management, and communication.

Balancing academics and extracurriculars

Balancing academics and extracurriculars is a crucial aspect of preparing academically for college. While it is important to prioritize your studies, being involved in extracurricular activities can also greatly benefit your college application.

When it comes to balancing academics and extracurriculars, it's essential to find a healthy middle ground. Striking a balance allows you to excel academically, while still participating in activities that interest you and showcase your unique talents.

To begin, start by choosing extracurricular activities that align with your passions and strengths. Rather than participating in numerous activities just for the sake of it, focus on quality over quantity. Admissions officers often look for students who demonstrate commitment and dedication in a few activities rather than those who have a long list of superficial involvements.

Once you have chosen your activities, time management becomes crucial. Prioritize your schoolwork by creating a schedule and setting aside specific study hours. By doing so, you can ensure that your academic performance remains strong while still having time to participate in your chosen activities.

One effective strategy for balancing your commitments is to integrate your extracurriculars into your academic routine. For example, if you are passionate about photography, consider joining the school yearbook staff or starting a photography club. This way, you can pursue your interests while also connecting them to your academic pursuits.

Additionally, taking on leadership roles within your extracurricular activities can be highly beneficial. Holding a leadership position demonstrates your ability to take initiative, collaborate with others, and manage responsibilities effectively. Colleges view leadership as a valuable trait, as it shows your potential for success both inside and outside of the classroom.

Remember, achieving a balance between academics and extracurriculars is not about sacrificing one for the other. Instead, it's about finding harmony between the two aspects of your life. Prioritize your studies, but also make time for activities that you are genuinely passionate about. By doing so, you can demonstrate to colleges that you are a well-rounded individual with a strong work ethic and a commitment to personal growth.

In the next chapter, we will explore the importance of standardized tests and how to effectively prepare for them. Stay tuned for expert insights, practical strategies, and real-world data analysis to help you navigate the college admission process successfully.

Chapter 4
Standardized Tests: SATs and ACTs

Overview of SAT and ACT Tests

Standardized tests like the SAT and ACT play a crucial role in the college application process. They provide colleges with a standardized measure of a student's academic abilities and allow admissions officers to compare applicants on a level playing field. In this section, we will explore the formats of these tests, how to prepare for them, and the implications of your scores on college admissions.

The SAT, administered by the College Board, is a widely recognized and accepted standardized test for college admissions in the United States. It consists of two main sections - Evidence-Based Reading and Writing, and Math

- and an optional essay section. The test is scored on a scale of 400 to 1600, with 1600 being the highest possible score. The SAT assesses critical thinking skills, problem-solving abilities, and knowledge of key concepts in math and English.

On the other hand, the ACT, administered by ACT, Inc., is an alternative standardized test that some colleges accept in lieu of the SAT. The ACT covers four main sections - English, Math, Reading, and Science - and also offers an optional essay section. The test is scored on a scale of 1 to 36, with 36 being the highest possible score. The ACT emphasizes knowledge-based questions more, testing what students have learned in their high school curriculum.

It is essential to research the colleges you are interested in to determine whether they prefer the SAT or ACT or accept both. Some colleges may have specific requirements, so it's crucial to familiarize yourself with their admissions policies.

Preparing for these standardized tests requires a combination of knowledge, skills, and strategies. Familiarizing yourself with the test format by studying sample questions and taking practice tests can help you become more comfortable with the types of questions you'll encounter. Additionally, investing time in reviewing content areas, such as math formulas or grammar rules, can help strengthen your overall performance. Many resources, such as books, online courses, and tutoring services, are available to assist you in your preparation.

Your scores on the SAT or ACT can significantly impact your college admissions prospects. Colleges use these scores to evaluate your academic readiness and potential for success. While a high score is advantageous, it's important to note that colleges also consider other factors, such as your GPA, extracurricular activities, essays, and letters of recommendation. Therefore, it's crucial to approach these tests with adequate preparation but also remember that they are just one piece of the college admissions puzzle.

In the following chapters, we will dive deeper into strategies for test preparation, explore tips to improve your performance on the SAT or ACT and discuss how to interpret your scores and use them to your advantage during the college application process. Understanding the significance of these standardized tests and effectively preparing for them will increase your chances of gaining admission to the college or university of your choice.

Preparing for standardized tests.

Preparing for standardized tests requires careful planning and diligent effort. It is crucial to approach these exams with a strategic mindset and utilize effective study techniques. This section will outline the essential steps to help you prepare for the SAT and ACT.

1. Understand the Format: Familiarize yourself with the structure and content of the tests. The SAT consists of sections in Reading, Writing and Language, Math (with and without a calculator), and an optional Essay. The ACT comprises sections in English, Math, Reading, Science, and an optional Writing portion. Knowing the format will help you identify your strengths and weaknesses.

2. Research College Preferences: Different colleges and universities have varying requirements and preferences when it comes to standardized tests. Some may have a preference for the SAT, while others may consider ACT scores. Take the time to research the admission policies of your target schools to ensure you are focusing your efforts on the right test.

3. Create a Study Plan: Develop a study schedule that allows for consistent and focused preparation. Allocate time for each section of the test, focusing on areas where you may need improvement. A well-structured study plan will help you stay organized and make the most of your study time.

4. Utilize Practice Materials: Practice tests and sample questions are invaluable resources in your test preparation journey. These materials will familiarize you with the types of questions and the overall test structure. They will also give you a sense of timing, enabling you to manage your time effectively during the exam.

5. Seek Additional Resources: Consider using additional resources such as study guides, online tutorials, and review books. These materials can provide further explanations, tips, and strategies to enhance your understanding of the test content. Make sure to choose reputable resources that align with the latest test formats.

6. Take Timed Practice Tests: Regularly take full-length practice tests under timed conditions to simulate the actual testing environment. This will improve your time management skills and help build endurance. Analyze your results to identify areas that need more attention and focus your efforts accordingly.

7. Review Content Areas: Dedicate time to review the content areas tested in the exams. In addition to practicing test questions, ensure a solid understanding of the concepts and skills required. Use study guides and practice materials to reinforce your knowledge in areas like grammar, reading comprehension, algebra, and geometry.

8. Engage in Test-Taking Strategies: Familiarize yourself with effective test-taking strategies. Learn to eliminate answer choices, guess strategically, and manage your time wisely. Understanding these strategies can significantly improve your performance and increase your chances of obtaining a higher score.

Remember, that standardized test scores are just one component of your college application. While they play a significant role, colleges also consider other factors such as your GPA, extracurricular activities, essays, and letters of recommendation. Keep your focus on achieving well-rounded excellence, both academically and personally, throughout your high school journey.

By following these steps and dedicating yourself to thorough preparation, you can approach the SAT and ACT with confidence and maximize your chances of success.

Understanding Test Formats and Scoring

In order to successfully prepare for the SAT and ACT, it is essential that students have a solid understanding of the test formats and scoring systems. Familiarizing oneself with these aspects will not only help in creating a study plan but also enable students to perform their best on test day.

The SAT consists of two main sections: Evidence-Based Reading and Writing (EBRW) and Math, with an optional Essay section. The EBRW section assesses critical reading, writing, and language skills through multiple-choice questions and a passage-based essay. The Math section evaluates math knowledge and problem-solving abilities.

The ACT, on the other hand, comprises four sections: English, Math, Reading, and Science, with an optional Writing section. The English section measures grammar and punctuation skills, while the Math section focuses on math concepts and problem-solving. The Reading section assesses reading comprehension, and the Science section evaluates scientific analysis and interpretation.

Both tests are administered in multiple-choice format, with the exception of the SAT Essay and ACT Writing sections. It is crucial for students to understand the time constraints for each section and effectively manage their time during the test.

Scoring for the SAT and ACT is also slightly different. The SAT is scored on a scale of 400-1600, with separate scores for EBRW and Math. The optional Essay is scored separately and does not contribute to the overall score. On the other hand, the ACT is scored on a scale of 1-36 for each section, and an average composite score is calculated from the four sections.

Understanding the scoring systems allows students to set realistic goals and gauge their performance. It is important to note that both tests are widely accepted by colleges and universities across the United States, and there is no definitive answer on which test is better. Students should research the preferences of their target colleges and determine which test aligns better with their strengths and preferences.

By familiarizing themselves with the formats and scoring systems of the SAT and ACT, students can strategically plan their study approach, allocate time for each section, and focus on areas that require improvement. It is crucial to practice with official practice materials and employ test-taking strategies to build confidence and maximize scores.

In the next segment, we will dive deeper into effective study strategies and resources that will aid students in achieving their desired scores on the SAT and ACT.

The role of test scores in college admissions

The role of test scores in college admissions cannot be overstated. Universities and colleges often consider standardized test scores as an essential part of the application process. These scores provide a measure of a student's academic abilities and act as a benchmark for comparison among applicants.

While it is true that test scores do not solely determine admission to colleges and universities, they hold considerable weight in the decision-making process. Admissions committees use test scores, together with other application materials such as GPA, essays, and extracurricular activities, to evaluate a student's potential and fit within their institution.

Standardized test scores provide colleges with a standardized and objective measure to compare students from different high schools, districts, and even countries. They allow colleges to assess applicants' readiness for rigorous academic programs and determine if students can thrive in the college environment.

It is important to note that different colleges and universities place varying levels of importance on test scores. Some highly selective institutions may prioritize test scores heavily, while others adopt a more holistic approach, considering a range of factors beyond just test performance. However, for most colleges, good test scores can enhance a student's competitiveness and increase their chances of admission.

To maximize their chances of admission, students should aim to achieve scores that align with their target colleges' average admitted student scores. Researching the average scores of admitted students at desired institutions can provide guidance on setting realistic score goals. In some cases, colleges may even publicly disclose the average test scores for their admitted students, making it easier for prospective applicants to gauge where they stand.

In addition to simply meeting the average score requirements, students should aim to achieve scores that demonstrate their academic capabilities and potential. Strong test scores can help applicants stand out in a competitive pool of candidates and showcase their abilities beyond just their grades.

It is worth mentioning that while test scores are pivotal for admission, they are not the sole indication of a student's abilities or potential success in college. Admission committees also take into account other aspects such as personal essays, letters of recommendation, extracurricular activities, and demonstrated passion or talent in specific areas.

While test scores are important, a comprehensive and well-rounded application is crucial. Students should strive to excel academically, participate in meaningful extracurricular activities, and showcase their unique qualities and experiences through their application materials. By doing so, they can present a holistic picture of their abilities and increase their chances of securing admission to their desired colleges and universities.

In the following chapters, we will dive deeper into strategies for test preparation and provide tips to help students achieve their best possible scores on standardized tests like the SAT and ACT. Additionally, we will explore alternative admission policies and institutions that do not require test scores. Stay tuned for valuable insights and advice to make your college application journey a successful one.

Chapter 5
Building a Strong Application

Crafting a compelling personal statement

Crafting a compelling personal statement is a crucial aspect of building a strong college application. This is your opportunity to showcase your unique qualities, experiences, and aspirations in a way that captures the attention of admissions officers.

To begin, reflect on your personal story and identify key moments or experiences that have shaped you. Think about the challenges you have overcome, the lessons you have learned, and the values that guide your life. These elements will form the foundation of your personal statement.

Start your personal statement with a captivating introduction that immediately grabs the reader's attention. Consider sharing a personal anecdote or a thought-provoking question that sets the stage for the rest of your essay. Remember, this is your chance to make a lasting impression, so make sure your introduction is compelling and engaging.

As you dive. into the body of your personal statement, be specific and provide concrete examples to support your claims. Avoid generalizations and clichés, instead, focus on telling your unique story. Use descriptive language to paint a vivid picture of your experiences and emotions. Admission officers want to understand who you are as a person, so be authentic and genuine in your writing.

Highlight your achievements and involvement in extracurricular activities, but don't simply list them. Instead, demonstrate the impact these experiences have had on your personal and intellectual growth. Discuss how they have shaped your values, skills, and future goals. Show the admissions committee your passion and dedication through specific anecdotes and examples.

In addition to showcasing your accomplishments, discuss any challenges you have faced and how you have overcome them. Admission officers recognize that resilience and perseverance are valuable traits, so sharing your struggles and growth can make your essay more compelling.

As you conclude your personal statement, reflect on what you have learned and how your experiences have prepared you for college. Emphasize the connections between your past accomplishments and your future aspirations. Tie everything together in a meaningful way, which leaves a lasting impression on the reader.

Remember to revise and edit your personal statement carefully. Seek feedback from trusted teachers, counselors, or mentors to ensure your essay is clear, concise, and error-free. Take the time to make every word count and ensure that your personal statement accurately represents who you are as a person.

Crafting a compelling personal statement is a challenging but rewarding process. By sharing your unique story, experiences, and aspirations, you can demonstrate to admissions officers why you are an exceptional candidate for their institution. Use this opportunity to stand out from the crowd and showcase your true potential.

Gathering strong letters of recommendation

Gathering strong letters of recommendation is another crucial aspect of building a strong college application. These letters provide insight into your character, work ethic, and potential for success in college. Here are some essential steps to follow when gathering letters of recommendation:

1. Choose the right recommenders: Select individuals who know you well and can speak to your strengths, skills, and accomplishments. This could include teachers, counselors, coaches, employers, or mentors. Consider their familiarity with your academic, extracurricular, or professional involvement.

2. Establish strong relationships: Building meaningful connections with potential recommenders is vital. Take the time to engage in class discussions, participate in extracurricular activities, seek guidance from your teachers, and demonstrate commitment in your various pursuits. This will enable your recommenders to write detailed and accurate letters that truly highlight your abilities.

3. Request letters in advance: Give your recommenders ample time to write your letters. It is considerate to approach them at least a month before the deadline, providing them with all necessary information such as application due dates, specific requirements, and submission instructions.

4. Provide necessary materials: To assist your recommenders in crafting compelling letters, offer them relevant information about your achievements, experiences, and aspirations. This can include your resume, personal statement, academic transcript, and any notable projects or awards you have received.

5. Clearly communicate your goals: Talk openly with your recommenders about your college aspirations, intended major or area of study, and the key qualities or experiences you hope they will emphasize. This will guide their writing and ensure that their letters align with your overall application narrative.

6. Follow up and express gratitude: After requesting your letters, make sure to express your appreciation to your recommenders for their time and effort. A thank-you note or email can go a long way in showing your gratitude. Additionally, keep them informed about your application outcomes as a gesture of respect and consideration.

Remember, gathering strong letters of recommendation requires careful planning and proactive engagement with your potential recommenders. By selecting the right individuals and nurturing meaningful relationships, you increase your chances of obtaining compelling letters that reinforce your application and set you apart from other candidates.

Showcasing extracurricular activities

Showcasing extracurricular activities is a vital part of building a strong college application. Admissions officers not only want to see academic achievement but also evidence of well-roundedness and personal growth outside of the classroom. In this section, we will explore effective strategies to highlight your extracurricular involvement and make a lasting impression on college admissions committees.

First and foremost, it's important to choose activities that you are genuinely passionate about. Admissions officers can easily spot when an applicant has joined clubs or organizations solely for the purpose of padding their resume. Instead, focus on activities that align with your interests, talents, and values. Whether it's playing a musical instrument, participating in community service projects, competing in sports, or engaging in leadership roles, be sure to highlight your dedication and growth in these areas.

When listing your extracurricular activities on your application, provide a clear and concise description of each one. Rather than simply stating the name of the club or organization, briefly explain your role and the impact you made. For example, if you were a member of a school newspaper, mention specific articles you wrote, any awards you received, and how your work contributed to the overall success of the publication.

Additionally, consider including any leadership positions or honors you have received within your extracurricular activities. This demonstrates your ability to take initiative, collaborate with others, and assume responsibility. Whether it's being elected as the president of a club or receiving recognition as the captain of a sports team, these achievements can set you apart from other applicants.

In order to showcase your extracurricular involvement even further, consider creating a supplemental resume or portfolio. This can be a document or online platform that provides more detailed information about your activities and accomplishments. Include photographs, videos, articles, or any other tangible evidence of your involvement. This not only helps admission officers visualize your experiences but also allows you to provide additional context and depth to your application.

Lastly, don't underestimate the power of reflection. Many colleges and universities value introspection and the ability to articulate personal growth. Take the time to think about how your extracurricular activities have shaped you as an individual, and contributed to your overall development. When writing your personal statement or during interviews, incorporate these meaningful experiences and their impacts on your life.

Remember, the goal is not to simply participate in as many activities as possible but rather to demonstrate your commitment, passion, and ability to make a difference. By showcasing your extracurricular activities effectively, you can enhance your application and increase your chances of getting accepted into the college or university of your dreams.

Overall Application Strategy and Tips

Crafting a compelling college application requires careful planning and attention to detail. In this section, we will discuss an overall application strategy that will help you stand out from the competition and increase your chances of acceptance into your desired colleges or universities.

1. Start Early: Give yourself plenty of time to prepare your application materials. Begin researching colleges and universities during your junior year of high school, as this will give you ample time to gather information and tailor your application accordingly.

2. Know Your Strengths: Before you start filling out applications, take the time to identify your strengths, passions, and accomplishments. Reflect on your academic achievements, extracurricular activities, and personal experiences that have shaped you. This self-reflection will help you present a holistic and authentic picture of who you are to admissions officers.

3. Develop a Strong Personal Statement: The personal statement is your chance to showcase your unique qualities and experiences. Spend time brainstorming and drafting a compelling essay that captures the attention of the readers. Be sure to focus on a specific topic or theme and provide concrete examples to support your claims.

4. Gather Impactful Letters of Recommendation: Selecting the right individuals to write your letters of recommendation is crucial. Choose teachers, coaches, or mentors who know you well and can speak to your abilities, character, and potential. Provide them with a clear understanding of your educational and career goals, and politely remind them of any key aspects they might consider including in their letters.

5. Showcase Extracurricular Activities: Admissions officers are not only interested in your academic achievements but also in the contributions you make outside the classroom. Highlight leadership positions, community service involvement, and any honors or awards you have received. Include clear descriptions and tangible evidence of your involvement to demonstrate the impact you have made in these activities.

6. Tailor Your Application to Each Institution: While it can be tempting to use the same application materials for all colleges and universities, take the time to customize each application to the specific institution. Research each college's mission, values, and programs, and adapt your personal statement and activities section to align with their expectations.

7. Seek Feedback and Proofread: Before submitting your application, seek feedback from teachers, counselors, or trusted adults. They can offer valuable insights and suggestions for improvement. Make sure to proofread

your application thoroughly for any grammar or spelling errors. Attention to detail is crucial in leaving a positive impression on admissions officers.

Remember, that the college application process is not solely based on grades and test scores. Admissions officers want to see who you are as a person and what you can contribute to their institution. By following these strategies and tips, you will be on your way to building a strong college application that showcases your unique qualities and increases your chances of getting into the college or university of your dreams.

Chapter 6
Financial Aid and Scholarships

Navigating financial aid options

Navigating financial aid options can be an overwhelming task for high school students, but with the right information and strategies, it is possible to secure the financial support you need for college. In this section, we will explore the different types of financial aid available and provide practical guidance on how to apply for scholarships and grants.

One of the first steps in the financial aid process is completing the Free Application for Federal Student Aid (FAFSA). This form collects important information about your family's income and assets to determine your eligibility for federal financial aid programs. It is essential to submit the FAFSA as soon as possible after October 1st of your senior year, as some types of aid have limited funds and are awarded on a first-come, first-served basis.

In addition to federal aid, many colleges and universities also offer institutional or merit-based scholarships. These scholarships are often awarded based on academic achievement, leadership potential, or specific talents. Researching and identifying the scholarships offered by your desired schools is a crucial step in maximizing your financial aid opportunities. Each scholarship may have its own application requirements and deadlines, so be sure to carefully review the instructions and submit all necessary materials on time.

It's important to keep in mind that scholarships can also be found outside of your chosen institution. Many private organizations, businesses, and foundations offer scholarships to high school students. Some scholarships are targeted towards specific fields of study or underserved communities. To find these opportunities, consider utilizing online scholarship search engines, exploring community resources, and reaching out to your school's college counselor or local organizations for guidance.

When applying for scholarships, it is crucial to pay attention to the application requirements and instructions. Some scholarships may require additional essays, letters of recommendation, or interviews. Take the time to tailor your applications to each scholarship and showcase your unique qualities and accomplishments. Remember, scholarships provide an opportunity to stand out from other applicants and demonstrate your potential.

Another form of financial aid worth considering is grants. Grants are typically need-based and do not require repayment. They can come from various sources, including the federal government, state governments, and private organizations. Similar to scholarships, grant applications may have specific criteria and deadlines. Be sure to thoroughly research and apply for grants that align with your financial needs and goals.

In conclusion, navigating financial aid options requires proactive research and planning. Start early and familiarize yourself with the various forms of financial aid available, including scholarships, grants, and federal aid programs. Take the time to complete the FAFSA accurately and on time, and diligently search for both institution-specific and outside scholarships. Keep track of application deadlines, requirements, and be sure to tailor your applications to showcase your unique qualities. By taking these steps, you can increase your chances of securing the financial support needed to pursue your college education.

Understanding Different Types of Scholarships

Scholarships are a valuable form of financial aid that can significantly reduce the cost of college education. They are awarded based on various criteria such as academic achievement, athletic ability, artistic talent, community involvement, or specific career aspirations. In this section, we will explore the different types of scholarships available to high school students in the United States.

1. Merit-Based Scholarships: These scholarships are awarded to students who have demonstrated exceptional academic achievements, leadership skills, or outstanding talents in a particular field. Merit-based scholarships can be offered by colleges and universities or by external organizations. To be eligible for these scholarships, students often must meet specific GPA requirements, provide letters of recommendation, and submit a personal statement or essay highlighting their accomplishments and goals.

2. Need-Based Scholarships: These scholarships are awarded to students who demonstrate significant financial need. Financial need is typically determined by evaluating the student's family income, assets, and overall financial situation. Need-based scholarships can be offered by both colleges and external organizations. To apply for these scholarships, students will need to fill out the Free

Application for Federal Student Aid (FAFSA) and provide any additional financial documentation required by the scholarship provider.

3. Athletic Scholarships: These scholarships are awarded to students who excel in a particular sport and can contribute to the athletic program of a college or university. Athletic scholarships are highly competitive and can be offered at both the Division I and Division II levels of the NCAA. Eligibility for athletic scholarships is determined by the student's athletic abilities and potential to compete at the collegiate level. It is important for student-athletes to work closely with their high school coaches and athletic advisors to identify opportunities and navigate the recruitment process.

4. Talent-Based Scholarships: These scholarships are awarded to students who excel in various artistic fields such as music, dance, theater, or visual arts. Talent-based scholarships can be offered by colleges, universities, or external organizations. Each scholarship may have its own specific requirements, such as auditions, portfolio submissions, or interviews. Students who are passionate about their artistic pursuits should research and explore scholarship opportunities relevant to their specific talents.

5. Community Service Scholarships: These scholarships recognize students who have made significant contributions to their communities through volunteer work and civic engagement. Many colleges and universities

offer scholarships to students with a demonstrated commitment to community service. To apply for these scholarships, students may need to provide documentation of their volunteer activities, letters of recommendation from community leaders, and personal statements describing their experiences and impact.

6. Career-Specific Scholarships: These scholarships are awarded to students who are pursuing a specific career path or field of study. They are often sponsored by professional associations, corporations, or government entities with the aim of encouraging students to pursue careers in high-demand fields. Examples of career-specific scholarships include those for STEM (Science, Technology, Engineering, and Mathematics) disciplines, healthcare, business, or education. Students interested in these fields should explore scholarship opportunities related to their career goals.

Understanding the different types of scholarships available is crucial for high school students seeking financial support for college. By researching and applying for scholarships that align with their strengths, talents, and goals, students can increase their chances of securing valuable funding and making their college dreams a reality.

Applying for financial aid and scholarships

Applying for financial aid and scholarships can be a daunting process, but with some guidance and preparation, it becomes more manageable. In this section, we will explore the steps involved in applying for financial aid and scholarships and provide practical strategies to increase your chances of securing funding for college.

1. Start Early:

It's never too early to start thinking about financial aid and scholarships. Begin by doing your research and familiarizing yourself with the various types of aid available. This will give you a better understanding of what options are out there and what you should be looking for.

2. Complete the FAFSA:

The Free Application for Federal Student Aid (FAFSA) is a crucial step in receiving financial aid from the government. It's essential to complete the FAFSA accurately and submit it before the deadline. The FAFSA will determine your eligibility for federal grants, loans, and work-study programs.

3. Research Scholarships:

There are numerous scholarships available to high school students, but finding the right ones can be overwhelming.

Take the time to research scholarships that align with your interests, talents, and achievements. Look for both national and local scholarships, as many organizations offer funding opportunities at the community level.

4. Pay Attention to Deadlines:

Missing scholarship application deadlines can result in missed opportunities, so it's crucial to stay organized and keep track of all the deadlines. Create a calendar or a spreadsheet to list the deadlines of the scholarships you want to apply for, along with the required documents.

5. Gather Required Documents:

Before applying for scholarships, ensure you have all the necessary documents ready. These may include your academic transcripts, recommendation letters, personal essays, and proof of financial need. Having these documents prepared in advance will make the application process smoother and more efficient.

6. Tailor Your Applications:

When applying for scholarships, take the time to tailor your applications to each specific opportunity. Pay attention to the scholarship requirements and answer the questions or prompts accordingly. Tailoring your applications shows effort and dedication, increasing your chances of being chosen as a recipient.

7. Seek Additional Financial Aid:

While scholarships are a valuable source of financial aid, they may not cover all your college expenses. Therefore, consider other options, such as grants, work-study programs, or low-interest student loans. Explore different avenues to ensure you secure enough funding to make your college education more affordable.

8. Maintain a Strong Academic Record:

Many scholarships take into account your academic performance, so it's crucial to maintain a strong GPA throughout high school. Strive for excellence in your coursework, participate in extracurricular activities, and foster positive relationships with your teachers. These efforts can provide you with valuable letters of recommendation and make you a more competitive applicant.

9. Don't Be Discouraged:

The process of applying for financial aid and scholarships can be competitive, and it's normal to face rejections along the way. Don't let these setbacks discourage you. Keep applying for opportunities that match your qualifications and interests, and remember that persistence pays off.

By following these steps and strategies, you'll be well-equipped to navigate the financial aid and scholarship application process. Remember always to stay organized, proactive, and informed, as this will greatly increase your chances of securing the financial support you need to pursue your college education.

Tips for Maximizing Financial Support

When it comes to financing your college education, there are a number of tips and strategies that can help you maximize the financial support available to you. Here are some key considerations to keep in mind:

Start Early: It's never too early to begin researching financial aid options and scholarships. Many scholarship programs have early application deadlines, so starting your search early will give you ample time to gather the necessary documents and complete the applications.

Complete the FAFSA: The Free Application for Federal Student Aid (FAFSA) is a crucial step in the financial aid process. By filling out this form, you will be considered for various federal student aid programs, including grants, loans, and work-study opportunities. Be sure to submit the FAFSA as early as possible to maximize your chances of receiving aid.

Research Scholarships: Scholarships are a valuable source of financial support, and there are numerous opportunities available to high school students. Take the time to research scholarships that align with your interests, achievements, and demographic background. Websites like Fastweb and

Scholarships.com can help you find scholarships that you may be eligible for.

Pay Attention to Deadlines: Missing scholarship deadlines can be a costly mistake. Mark important deadlines on your calendar and create a system to keep track of application requirements. Plan ahead and give yourself plenty of time to gather all necessary documents and complete the application process.

Tailor Your Applications: When applying for scholarships, it's important to tailor your applications to match the specific criteria and requirements of each scholarship. Take the time to read and understand the application guidelines, and customize your responses accordingly. Highlight your achievements, extracurricular activities, and personal experiences that align with the scholarship's mission or requirements.

Seek Additional Financial Aid: In addition to scholarships, explore other financial aid options such as grants, work-study programs, and tuition reimbursement. Contact your high school guidance counselor or college financial aid office for information on additional avenues for financial support.

Maintain a Strong Academic Record: Many scholarships and financial aid programs have academic requirements, so it's important to maintain a strong academic record throughout high school. Stay focused, study diligently, and seek help when needed to ensure that your grades remain competitive.

Don't Be Discouraged by Rejections: It's common to face rejections when applying for scholarships. Don't let this discourage you. Use each rejection as an opportunity to learn and improve your future applications. Remember that there are numerous scholarships available, and persistence pays off.

By following these tips, you can increase your chances of maximizing the financial support available to you for your college education. Remember to start early, complete the FAFSA, research scholarships, pay attention to deadlines, tailor your applications, seek additional financial aid, maintain a strong academic record, and not be discouraged by rejections. With careful planning and perseverance, you'll be able to secure the funding you need to achieve your educational goals.

Chapter 7
College Visits and Interviews

The importance of college visits

Visiting colleges before making a decision on where to apply is a crucial step in the college application process. It provides students with the opportunity to get a firsthand look at the campus, the surrounding environment, and the overall atmosphere of the institution.

During a college visit, students can explore the campus facilities, such as classrooms, libraries, laboratories, and dormitories. It allows them to gain a sense of the size of the campus, the available resources, and the quality of the facilities. Additionally, students can attend information sessions and take part in campus tours led by current students. These activities provide valuable insights into the academic programs, extracurricular activities, and support services offered by the college or university.

One of the benefits of college visits is the chance to interact with current students and faculty members. Engaging in conversations with students who are pursuing similar academic interests can shed light on the campus culture and student life. This firsthand information can help students understand whether the institution aligns with their preferences and goals.

Moreover, college visits offer the opportunity to meet with admissions representatives or attend college fairs. These interactions allow students to make a positive impression and demonstrate their interest in the institution, which can contribute to a strong college application.

While college visits can be time-consuming and expensive, many students find them to be a worthwhile investment of time and resources. Research has shown that students who visit colleges are more likely to be accepted and have higher graduation rates compared to those who do not visit. Additionally, visiting campuses can help students narrow down their college choices, ensuring they make a well-informed decision.

To make the most of college visits, it is important for students to prepare in advance. Researching the college or university beforehand can help students ask relevant questions and engage in meaningful conversations during their visit. It is also helpful to schedule appointments with professors, coaches, or advisors in advance if students have specific areas of interest or need additional support.

In conclusion, college visits are an essential part of the college application process. They provide students with valuable insights into the campus culture, academic programs, and student life. By investing time and effort in visiting colleges, students can make informed decisions about where to apply and increase their chances of being admitted to a good-fit institution.

Maximizing the Campus Visit Experience

A college visit is more than just a tour of a campus; it's an opportunity for high school students to immerse themselves in the college atmosphere, get a feel for the campus culture, and gain valuable insights that can inform their decision-making process. To make the most of this experience, it's important to approach it with a plan and a set of strategies that will help you maximize your time and interactions.

1. Research, Research, Research: Before setting foot on campus, do your homework. Take the time to thoroughly research the college or university you'll be visiting. Familiarize yourself with the institution's academic departments, majors offered, extracurricular activities, and any specific programs or initiatives that pique your interest. Understanding the college's mission, values, and

unique features will allow you to ask more informed questions during your visit.

2. Plan Ahead: Contact the admissions office and inquire about any scheduled information sessions, campus tours, or meetings with faculty members or current students. Plan your visit accordingly, ensuring that you have ample time to explore the campus, attend presentations, and engage in conversations with faculty and staff.

3. Ask the Right Questions: Prepare a list of questions beforehand, focusing on areas that are important to you. This could include academic advising, internship opportunities, study abroad programs, campus resources, or anything else that aligns with your goals and interests. Be proactive in seeking out the information you need to make an informed decision.

4. Engage with Current Students: Interacting with current students can provide valuable insights into the college experience. Take advantage of opportunities to meet with students who share your intended major or extracurricular interests. Ask about their personal experiences, what they love about the college, and any challenges they may have faced. Their perspectives can give you a sense of whether the college is the right fit for you.

5. Explore the Surrounding Area: The college is not just the campus; it's also the surrounding community. Take some time to explore the town or city where the college is

located. Consider whether the location offers the kind of environment in which you can thrive, both academically and personally.

6. Take Notes and Reflect: Throughout your visit, take notes on your observations, conversations, and general impressions. Afterward, set aside time to reflect on your experience. Compare and contrast the pros and cons of each institution you visit, considering factors such as academic programs, campus facilities, student support services, and overall fit with your goals and values.

By approaching college visits in a structured and prepared manner, you can make the most out of these opportunities. Remember, the goal is to gather as much relevant information as possible to make an informed decision about your future education.

Preparing for college interviews

Preparing for college interviews is a crucial step in the application process. Interviews provide students with the opportunity to showcase their personality, interests, and goals, and can greatly influence the admissions decision. To make the most of this opportunity, it is important to be well-prepared and confident.

One key aspect of preparing for college interviews is conducting thorough research on the institution. Familiarize yourself with the college's mission, values, and academic programs. Read about notable faculty members, recent research initiatives, and any specific areas of focus that align with your interests. This knowledge will not only impress the interviewer but also help you tailor your responses to demonstrate your genuine interest in the institution.

Another important step is to practice your interviewing skills. You can do this by participating in mock interviews with a guidance counselor, teacher, or even a family member. Practice answering common interview questions and consider your responses in advance. Reflect on your experiences, accomplishments, and goals, and think about how they align with the college's values and mission. By doing so, you will be better equipped to articulate your thoughts during the actual interview.

In addition to practicing your responses, it's also essential to develop strong communication skills. Pay attention to your body language, maintain eye contact, and speak clearly and confidently. Practice active listening by nodding and responding to the interviewer's questions or comments. These non-verbal cues show your engagement and interest in the conversation.

During the interview, it is crucial to be yourself and showcase your authentic personality. Remember that the interviewer wants to get to know you as an individual, so don't be afraid to share personal anecdotes or experiences that are relevant to the conversation. Be honest and genuine in your answers, and avoid providing scripted or rehearsed responses.

Furthermore, it's important to come prepared with thoughtful questions to ask the interviewer. This demonstrates your interest in the institution and allows you to gather additional information to help you make an informed decision. Ask about specific academic programs, research opportunities, extracurricular activities, or anything else that aligns with your interests and goals. Remember, the interview is also an opportunity for you to assess whether the college is a good fit for you.

Lastly, always remember to send a thank-you note or email to the interviewer after the interview. This small gesture reinforces your interest in the college and demonstrates your professionalism and gratitude.

By following these tips and preparing thoroughly for college interviews, you will increase your chances of making a positive impression on the admissions committee and ultimately securing a spot at your desired college or university.

How visits and interviews impact your application

College visits and interviews are an essential part of the college application process. Not only do they allow students to learn more about the institution and determine if it's a good fit for their academic and personal goals, but they also provide an opportunity to make a positive impression on the admissions committee.

When visiting a college, it's crucial to take advantage of the various resources available. Attend information sessions and campus tours to get a sense of the campus culture, facilities, and academic programs offered. Take note of the campus layout, explore the classrooms, libraries, dormitories, and any other areas that interest you. This immersive experience will help you envision yourself as a student at the institution.

While on campus, try to schedule an interview if it's offered. College interviews provide a unique chance to showcase your personality, highlight your accomplishments, and express your interest in the institution. It's an opportunity for the admissions committee to get to know you beyond your application. Make sure to dress professionally, maintain good eye contact, and exude confidence throughout the interview process.

To prepare for a college interview, research the institution thoroughly. Familiarize yourself with the college's mission and values, academic programs, extracurricular activities, and current events. This knowledge will help you show genuine interest during the interview and ask thoughtful questions. Additionally, practice common interview questions and prepare your responses to ensure you can articulate your strengths, goals, and reasons for choosing the college.

During the interview, be authentic and true to yourself. Admissions committees seek students who will contribute positively to their campus community, and showcasing your true personality will help them gauge your fit. Avoid memorizing scripted answers and instead focus on expressing your genuine thoughts and experiences.

After the interview, send a thank-you note or email to the interviewer. This gesture demonstrates that you appreciate their time and reinforces your interest in the institution. Keep the note concise, polite, and personalized, highlighting key aspects of the interview or mentioning any specific topics that resonated with you.

Remember, your college visit and interview are not only evaluative for the college but also give you an opportunity to evaluate the college. Pay attention to how you feel on campus and if the atmosphere aligns with your values and aspirations. Use the experience to gather insights that will help you make an informed decision during the application process.

By making the most of college visits and interviews, you can greatly impact your application. Showcasing your genuine interest, preparation, and ability to connect with the institution will leave a lasting impression on the admissions committee. So take advantage of these opportunities and put your best foot forward as you strive to secure a spot at your desired college or university.

Chapter 8
Choosing the Right College

Factors to consider when choosing a college:

Choosing the right college is a critical decision that will shape your future. To make an informed choice, it is essential to evaluate various factors that align with your goals and values. Here are key considerations to keep in mind:

1. Location: Determine whether you prefer a college close to home or are open to exploring new areas. Consider the climate, surrounding community, and proximity to amenities that are important to you.

2. Size: Think about the size of the college that suits your preferred learning environment. Larger universities offer

a wide range of academic programs and extracurricular activities, while smaller colleges often foster a close-knit community and personalized attention.

3. Academic Programs: Research the academic departments and programs offered by each college. Look for institutions with strong programs in your intended field of study. Consider the curriculum, faculty expertise, and available resources.

4. Campus Culture: Explore the campus culture and student life. Consider the activities, clubs, and organizations that align with your interests. Look for colleges that provide a supportive and inclusive environment where you can thrive personally and academically.

5. Cost and Financial Aid: Evaluate the cost of tuition, fees, and living expenses. Consider your financial situation and whether you qualify for scholarships, grants, or financial aid. Keep in mind that attending an out-of-state college might incur higher expenses.

6. Opportunities for Growth: Consider the opportunities for internships, research projects, study abroad programs, and career services offered by the college. These experiences can enhance your education and provide valuable insights into your future career path.

7. Graduation and Retention Rates: Examine the college's graduation rates and the percentage of students who return

after their first year. Higher graduation and retention rates are indicative of a supportive and engaging academic environment.

8. Alumni Network and Job Placement: Look into the college's alumni network and the success of its graduates in finding jobs or pursuing advanced degrees. A strong alumni network can provide valuable connections and resources for future opportunities.

Remember, choosing a college is a personal decision, and what works for one student may not work for another. Take the time to visit campuses, talk to current students, and reflect on your priorities. By considering these factors, you will be better equipped to make an informed decision that sets you on the path to a successful college experience.

Assessing academic programs and faculty

Assessing academic programs and faculty is a crucial step in choosing the right college. It is essential for students to consider the quality and reputation of the programs they are interested in, as well as the expertise and qualifications of the faculty members who will be teaching and mentoring them.

When evaluating academic programs, students should look for a variety of majors and minors that align with their interests and career goals. They should also consider the depth and breadth of the curriculum, including the availability of advanced courses, research opportunities, and experiential learning options such as internships or study abroad programs.

To assess the quality of a college's academic programs, students can utilize resources such as college rankings, accreditation agencies, and alumni testimonials. Rankings, such as those published by U.S. News & World Report, provide insights into the overall reputation and strength of different colleges and universities. However, it is important to note that rankings should not be the sole determining factor in college selection.

Another important consideration is the faculty. Students should research the qualifications and experience of the faculty members within their intended departments or areas of study. This can be done by reviewing faculty profiles on college websites, reading publications or research papers authored by faculty members, or reaching out to current students or alumni for their perspectives.

Additionally, students should consider the faculty-to-student ratio, as this can impact the level of personalized attention and interaction they will receive. Smaller ratios generally indicate more opportunities for individualized instruction and mentorship.

When visiting college campuses, it can be helpful to schedule meetings or informational sessions with faculty members in prospective areas of study. This allows students to ask questions, gain insights into the department's resources and support systems, and assess the faculty's enthusiasm for teaching and mentoring students.

Overall, assessing academic programs and faculty is a crucial part of choosing the right college. By considering the quality and reputation of the programs and faculty members, students can ensure that they will receive a rigorous and enriching educational experience that aligns with their goals and aspirations.

Understanding campus culture and student life

In addition to academic programs and faculty, another crucial aspect to consider when choosing the right college is understanding the campus culture and student life. While the academic component is undoubtedly important, the overall college experience goes beyond classroom learning.

Campus culture refers to the social atmosphere, values, and traditions that exist within a college community. It encompasses everything from extracurricular activities and clubs to dorm life and campus events. Therefore, it is essential to assess whether the campus culture aligns with your interests, beliefs, and goals.

To gain insight into the campus culture, there are various strategies that can be employed. One effective method is attending college fairs and information sessions where representatives from different colleges provide details about their campus environment. These events offer an opportunity to engage in conversations, ask questions, and get a feel for the ethos of each institution.

Another valuable resource for understanding campus culture is talking to current students or recent alumni. Their firsthand experiences can give you a glimpse into the day-to-day life on campus, the relationships between students and faculty, and the overall student satisfaction. You can reach out through social media platforms, attend alumni events, or even schedule campus visits to meet and interact with students.

During campus visits, pay close attention to the atmosphere on campus. Observe how students interact with one another, whether there is a sense of community, and if the campus facilities support a vibrant student life. Take note of the clubs, organizations, and extracurricular opportunities available, as these can greatly enhance your college experience.

Additionally, consider the location of the college and how it might shape the campus culture. Different regions and cities offer unique opportunities and experiences. Some colleges may be situated in bustling urban areas, while others may be in more rural or suburban settings. Think about whether you prefer the energy and diversity of a city or the tranquility and close-knit community of a small town.

Furthermore, it is crucial to evaluate the demographic makeup of the student body. Is it diverse and inclusive, allowing for exposure to different perspectives and cultures? Consider how this aligns with your own values and goals for personal growth.

While academic programs may be the primary reason for attending college, student life plays a significant role in shaping your overall experience. By understanding the campus culture and evaluating the available student activities, you can ensure that you find a college where you will thrive both academically and personally.

Remember, choosing the right college is not solely about academics; it is about finding a community that supports your growth and allows you to pursue your passions outside the classroom. By considering campus culture and student life, you will be well on your way to finding a college that is the perfect fit for you.

Balancing Quality and Cost in College Selection

Choosing the right college involves considering both the quality of education and the cost associated with attending. While everyone wants to attend a prestigious and highly respected institution, it's essential to make sure that the investment is financially feasible.

When evaluating colleges, it's crucial to assess the value you will receive in return for the tuition fees. Look for colleges that have a strong reputation academically and offer programs that align with your interests and career goals. Consider factors like faculty expertise, research opportunities, internship placements, and alumni success. These indicators can help gauge the quality of education you'll receive.

However, it's equally important to evaluate the cost of attending college. Many students and their families rely on financial aid or scholarships to make college affordable. When comparing colleges, take into account the financial aid packages offered, including grants, scholarships, and work-study opportunities. Look at the average debt burden of students graduating from each college and the availability of manageable repayment plans.

Additionally, consider the cost of living in the location where the college is situated. Some areas have a higher cost of living, which can impact expenses beyond tuition fees. Compare housing options, transportation costs, and the availability of part-time job opportunities in the vicinity of the college.

To balance quality and cost effectively, you may need to make compromises. Consider the financial implications of attending a prestigious institution versus a more affordable one. Remember, many excellent colleges offer a quality education at a more reasonable price.

Another aspect to consider is the long-term return on investment. Research the career prospects and earning potential for graduates of the colleges you are considering. Look into job placement rates, starting salaries, and the reputation of the college among potential employers. This information will help you assess whether the college's cost is justified by future career opportunities.

Various tools and resources can assist in comparing college costs. Take advantage of websites that provide detailed information on tuition fees, financial aid options, and student loan repayment calculators. These tools can help you estimate the actual cost of attending different colleges and determine the feasible options for you and your family.

Evaluating quality and cost simultaneously will allow you to make an informed decision when choosing the right college. Remember that the ultimate goal is to find an institution that provides an excellent education and cultivates personal growth while remaining financially manageable.

Chapter 9
The Application Timeline

Early high school preparation

Early high school preparation is crucial for students who aspire to attend a good college or university. During these formative years, students can lay a strong foundation for their academic and extracurricular pursuits. By strategically planning their coursework, engaging in meaningful activities, and seeking guidance from mentors, students can enhance their chances of securing admission to their dream college.

In the freshman and sophomore years of high school, students should focus on building a strong academic record. They should enroll in a rigorous course load that includes core subjects such as English, math, science, and social studies. It is also advisable for students to take elective courses that align with their interests and potentially showcase their strengths. This way, students can begin to explore various fields of study and develop their passion for learning.

Furthermore, students should take advantage of opportunities to excel outside the classroom. Participating in clubs, sports teams, community service, or other extracurricular activities can demonstrate leadership skills and a commitment to personal growth. These activities can also help students develop important qualities such as teamwork, time management, and resilience.

As students progress into their junior year, it is crucial to start thinking more seriously about college. This includes researching potential colleges and universities that align with their interests and goals. They should consider factors like size, location, academic programs, and campus culture when compiling a list of prospective schools.

In addition, students should use their junior year to prepare for standardized tests. Most colleges require either the SAT or ACT, and strong scores can greatly enhance a student's application. Preparing for these exams may involve taking practice tests, enrolling in test prep courses, or seeking guidance from a school counselor.

During the summer between junior and senior year, students should consider pursuing summer programs, internships, or volunteer opportunities related to their academic interests. These experiences can provide valuable real-world exposure and enhance a student's resume. Additionally, students may want to start brainstorming and drafting their personal statements or essays that will be required as part of their college applications.

Finally, as senior year begins, students should finalize their college list and create a timeline for completing applications. This includes submitting transcripts, requesting letters of recommendation from teachers or counselors, and preparing for any interviews or admissions exams.

In summary, early high school preparation is essential for students aiming to attend a good college or university. By focusing on academic excellence, exploring interests through extracurricular activities, and starting the college research process early, students can set themselves up for success in the competitive college application process.

Junior Year Strategies

Junior year is a crucial time for high school students as they begin to solidify their college plans. During this period, students can take significant steps towards creating a strong college application. Here are some strategies to consider during junior year:

1. Maintain a strong academic record: Colleges heavily consider a student's junior year grades, so it's essential to stay focused and perform well academically. Take challenging courses that align with your interests and future goals, and seek help or extra support if needed.

2. Prepare for standardized tests: The SAT or ACT are important factors in college admissions. Start preparing for these exams by taking practice tests, enrolling in test prep courses, or working with a tutor. Devote time regularly to study and review different test-taking strategies to improve your scores.

3. Get involved in extracurricular activities: College's value well-rounded students who are actively involved in their school and community. Continue participating in extracurricular activities that align with your interests and passions, and consider taking on leadership roles. Seek out new opportunities to showcase your abilities and make a positive impact.

4. Explore college options: Junior year is an ideal time to start researching colleges and universities. Consider factors such as location, academic programs, size, campus culture, and extracurricular opportunities. Attend college fairs, visit campuses, and talk to current college students or alumni to gather information and insights.

5. Develop relationships with teachers and mentors: Cultivate strong relationships with your teachers and

guidance counselors who can provide guidance and write recommendation letters for your college applications. Seek their advice on course selection, extracurricular involvement, and the overall college application process.

6. Begin compiling a list of potential colleges: Using the information gathered during your research, start creating a list of colleges that align with your academic and personal goals. Include a range of reach, match, and safety schools to increase your options.

7. Plan campus visits: Visiting college campuses provides invaluable first-hand experience and helps you determine if a college is a good fit. Arrange campus tours and information sessions, and consider attending college open house events or overnight visits if possible. Take notes during each visit to compare and evaluate the different campuses later.

8. Start preparing your resume: Begin creating a comprehensive resume that highlights your academic achievements, extracurricular activities, volunteer work, awards, and any other relevant experiences. This will serve as a foundation for your college applications and make it easier to accurately portray your accomplishments.

By following these strategies, high school juniors can lay a solid foundation for a successful college application process. Taking proactive measures during this crucial year will set them up for success as they embark on the next phase of their educational journey.

Senior year: Finalizing and Submitting Applications

Senior year is an exciting and challenging time for high school students. It marks the culmination of years of hard work, determination, and preparation. As a senior, you have now reached the stage where you will be putting all your efforts into finalizing and submitting your college applications. This chapter will guide you through the crucial steps involved in this process, ensuring that you present yourself in the best possible light to prospective colleges and universities.

1. Review Your College List: Begin by revisiting your list of potential colleges and universities. Consider factors such as academic fit, location, campus culture, and financial aid opportunities. Narrow down your choices to a manageable number, typically around five to ten institutions.

2. Finalize Your Application Strategy: Once you have your college list, it's essential to devise an application strategy. Determine whether you will apply through early decision, early action, regular decision, or a combination of these options. Understand the deadlines and requirements for each application type.

3. Verify Admission Requirements: Thoroughly research and understand the admission requirements for each college on your list. Review the average GPA, standardized test scores, extracurricular activities, essays, and recommendations needed for admission. Ensure that you meet or exceed these requirements.

4. Request Recommendation Letters: Ideally, you should have established strong relationships with teachers, mentors, and counselors throughout high school. Approach them respectfully and request recommendation letters well in advance of the application deadlines. Provide them with a comprehensive resume and any necessary forms.

5. Craft your Personal Statement and Essays: The personal statement and supplemental essays are your opportunity to showcase your unique qualities, experiences, and aspirations. Take the time to brainstorm, draft, revise, and edit these pieces. Seek feedback from teachers, mentors, and family members to ensure they truly reflect your voice.

6. Complete the Common Application: Many colleges and universities utilize the Common Application, which allows you to apply to multiple schools using a single form. Familiarize yourself with the Common Application and complete it accurately and thoughtfully. Pay close attention to the essay prompts and requirements.

7. Fine-tune Your Resume: Update your comprehensive resume to include all your achievements, activities, community service, and work experiences. Be sure to highlight your leadership roles, unique skills, and any awards or honors you have received. Make it a concise and visually appealing document.

8. Submit Standardized Test Scores: If you haven't already done so, send your official SAT or ACT scores to the colleges on your list. Double-check each institution's requirements and deadlines for test score submission. Consider taking tests again if you believe your scores can be improved.

9. Seek Financial Aid: If you require financial assistance, take the necessary steps to complete the Free Application for Federal Student Aid (FAFSA) and any additional institution-specific financial aid forms. Research scholarships, grants, and work-study opportunities to help fund your college education.

10. Stay Organized and Meet Deadlines: Finally, maintain a detailed calendar or planner to keep track of important application deadlines, submission materials, and interviews. Create a system that ensures you submit all required documents and fees on time for each institution.

As a high school senior, the college application process is both a significant milestone and a defining moment in your academic journey. Embrace the process, stay focused, and trust in the preparation you have undertaken throughout your high school years. With careful planning, attention to detail, and a strong work ethic, you are on your way to achieving your goal of attending a good college or university.

After submission: waiting and decision-making

Once all the college applications have been submitted, high school seniors enter a period of anticipation and uncertainty. This waiting period, which can last several weeks or even months, can be a time of stress and anxiety for students and their families. In this segment, we will explore strategies for managing this waiting period effectively and making informed decisions when acceptance letters start to arrive.

First and foremost, it is important to remember that the college admissions process is highly competitive, and not all students will receive acceptances from their top-choice schools. It is essential to have a realistic mindset and be prepared for different outcomes. Instead of fixating solely on a single dream school, maintain an open mind and consider a range of options.

During this waiting period, it is also crucial to continue focusing on academics and maintain strong grades. Colleges often request mid-year or final transcripts, and a decline in grades could potentially impact admissions decisions. Keep up with coursework, seek help when needed, and stay engaged in your education.

While waiting, it may be tempting to constantly check the mail or refresh your email inbox, but it is essential to strike a balance between staying informed and becoming consumed by the process. Create a system for tracking the status of your applications and important deadlines. This could be a spreadsheet or a digital calendar, whichever works best for you. This way, you won't miss any updates or opportunities to provide additional information if needed.

Remember, too, that acceptance or rejection letters do not define your worth or potential. College admissions decisions are influenced by a myriad of factors, many of which are beyond your control. Instead of dwelling on rejections, focus on the positive aspects of your application and acknowledge the effort you put into the process.

When acceptance letters start to arrive, carefully evaluate each offer. Consider factors such as financial aid packages, location, campus culture, academic programs, and resources available for your intended major. Take the time to visit campuses, attend admitted student events, and talk to current students to gain a better understanding of each institution.

If you are fortunate to receive multiple offers, weigh the pros and cons of each option and prioritize what is most important to you. Remember, you have the ability to negotiate financial aid packages or request additional scholarships, so don't be afraid to advocate for yourself.

In making the final decision, trust your instincts but also seek guidance from mentors, parents, and college counselors. They can provide valuable perspectives and help you navigate through the decision-making process.

Once you have accepted an offer and made a deposit, remember to inform other colleges of your decision promptly. This allows them to offer admission or financial aid resources to other deserving students.

By approaching the waiting period with grace and maintaining a level-headed approach to decision-making, high school seniors can navigate this final phase of the college application process successfully. Remember that the journey doesn't end with acceptance; it's just the beginning of an exciting new chapter in your educational journey.

Chapter 10
Dealing with Rejection and Waitlists

Coping with college rejections

Coping with college rejections can be a challenging experience for high school students, but it is important to remember that rejection letters do not define your worth or potential. While it may be disheartening to receive a rejection, it is crucial to maintain a positive mindset and focus on alternative options.

One effective strategy for coping with rejection is to allow yourself to feel disappointed and acknowledge your emotions. It is completely normal to feel upset or frustrated when you receive a rejection letter, as you have likely invested a significant amount of time and effort into your college applications. Give yourself permission to process these emotions, but also remember that setbacks are a natural part of life.

Instead of dwelling on the rejection, try to shift your focus to other colleges that have offered you admission. Take the time to carefully evaluate each offer and consider factors such as financial aid, location, academic programs, and campus culture. It might be helpful to create a pros and cons list for each school and discuss your options with trusted mentors or counselors.

If you find that you did not receive any acceptance letters or that the options available to you are not ideal, consider alternative pathways to further your education. Community colleges, for example, can provide an excellent foundation for transferring to a four-year institution later on. Exploring gap year programs, internships, or volunteering opportunities can also be fruitful experiences that will enhance your college application in the future.

During this time, it is important to stay motivated and engaged in your education. Continue to maintain strong grades and participate in extracurricular activities that align with your interests and goals. Remember that colleges often request updated transcripts, so it is essential to keep your academic performance consistent.

Finally, try to approach the college application process with resilience and maintain a level-headed perspective. Rejections and waitlists are not indicative of your abilities, but rather the result of a highly competitive and subjective process. Trust in your own abilities and have confidence in the unique qualities you bring to the table.

By implementing these strategies, you will be better equipped to cope with college rejections and move forward with a clear and determined mindset.

Understanding the waitlist process

Being placed on a waitlist can feel like a mix of hope and uncertainty. It's important to understand the waitlist process and how to navigate it effectively. In this section, we will dive into the key aspects of wait listing and provide you with practical strategies to increase your chances of admission.

1. Stay positive and maintain enthusiasm: Receiving a waitlist notification can be disheartening, but remember that it is not a rejection. Many students who were initially waitlisted have successfully gained admission to their desired college. Stay positive and maintain your enthusiasm for attending that institution.

2. Submit any additional materials: If the college allows it, consider submitting additional materials to bolster your application. This could be an updated resume, recent achievements, or a well-crafted letter expressing your continued interest in the school and why you believe you would be a good fit.

3. Confirm your interest: It is crucial to let the college know that you are still interested in attending if a spot becomes available. Write a formal letter or email expressing your continued interest in the institution and how it aligns with your academic and personal goals.

4. Keep in touch with the admissions office: Regularly communicate and inquire about any updates or changes to the waitlist status. Be respectful and professional in your correspondence, showing genuine interest without becoming a nuisance.

5. Pursue alternative options: While waiting for a decision from the waitlisted college, continue to explore other possibilities and accept offers from other schools you have been admitted to. It's important to have backup plans in case you are not ultimately admitted from the waitlist.

6. Consider an appeal: In some cases, you may have the option to appeal the admission decision. However, be aware that the chance of success is relatively low, and it should only be pursued if you believe there was a significant error or misunderstanding in your application evaluation.

7. Stay focused and committed: While waiting for a final decision, maintain your academic performance and involve yourself in meaningful extracurricular activities. Colleges want to see that you are continuing to grow and

excel, so demonstrate your commitment to personal and intellectual development.

Remember, the waitlist process is unpredictable, and there are no guarantees. However, by following these strategies, you can maximize your chances of being admitted from the waitlist. Stay positive, keep exploring alternative options, and continue to work towards your goals.

Strategies for being proactive while on a waitlist:

While receiving a waitlist notification can be disappointing, it doesn't mean the end of your college dreams. It's important to remain proactive and take strategic steps to increase your chances of eventually gaining admission to the college or university of your choice. Here are some strategies to consider:

1. Stay positive and resilient: It's natural to feel discouraged after being placed on a waitlist, but it's important to stay positive and maintain your focus. Remember that being waitlisted means the college sees your potential and is considering your application seriously. Use this time to reflect on your accomplishments and remind yourself of your strengths.

2. Submit additional materials: Take advantage of the opportunity to submit additional materials to strengthen your application. This could include updated grades, new

test scores, or additional recommendation letters. However, be cautious not to overwhelm the admissions office with unnecessary information. Only submit materials that genuinely add value to your application.

3. Confirm your interest: Show the college that you are still interested and sincerely want to attend if given the opportunity. Write a thoughtful letter or email expressing your continued interest in the school and explaining why you believe it is the right fit for you. Highlight specific aspects of the institution that align with your academic and personal goals.

4. Stay in touch with the admissions office: Establish a respectful and professional relationship with the admissions office. This can be done through periodic emails or phone calls to express your continued interest in the school and inquire about any updates regarding the waitlist process. However, be mindful not to contact them excessively or become a nuisance.

5. Pursue alternative options: While waiting for a decision from your preferred college, it's crucial to pursue alternative options simultaneously. Research and apply to other colleges that align with your interests and goals. This ensures that you have backup plans in the event you are not admitted from the waitlist.

6. Consider an appeal: Depending on the college's policies, you may have the option to appeal their decision. If you

believe there were extenuating circumstances or new information that was not initially included in your application, you can prepare an appeal letter explaining the situation and why you believe it warrants reconsideration. However, be cautious with this option, as not all colleges accept appeals.

7. Stay focused on personal and academic growth: While waiting for the final decision, continue to excel academically and engage in activities that demonstrate your commitment to personal development. This can include taking challenging courses, participating in extracurricular activities, and pursuing meaningful experiences outside the classroom.

Remember, being waitlisted doesn't mean a rejection, but it does require you to be proactive and assertive. By implementing these strategies, you can increase your chances of being admitted from the waitlist while also exploring other opportunities that may be available to you.

Developing alternative plans and options

When faced with the possibility of rejection or waitlist status, it is important to develop alternative plans and options to ensure that you have a backup plan and don't feel discouraged. Here are some strategies to consider:

1. Research and Explore Different Colleges: Take the time to research other colleges and universities that align with

your interests and goals. Look for schools that offer similar programs in your desired field of study or have a strong reputation in that area. Keep an open mind and be willing to explore different options.

2. Consider Community College: Community colleges can be a great stepping stone to a four-year university. These institutions often offer lower tuition costs and provide opportunities for academic and personal growth. Take advantage of transfer programs that allow you to seamlessly transfer credits to a four-year institution after completing your associate degree.

3. Look into Gap Year Programs: If you are not ready to jump straight into college, consider taking a gap year to pursue other interests and gain life experiences. There are various gap year programs that offer structured opportunities for travel, volunteer work, internships, or career exploration. These experiences can help you develop valuable skills and give you a fresh perspective before starting college.

4. Explore Online or Distance Learning: With advancements in technology, online or distance learning has become a viable option for many students. These programs offer flexibility and convenience, allowing you to pursue your education at your own pace and from the comfort of your own home. Be sure to research reputable online institutions and verify their accreditation.

5. Consider International Options: If you have always dreamed of studying abroad, now might be the time to explore international options. Many countries offer high-quality educational programs, often at a lower cost, and provide a unique cultural experience. Research universities in countries that interest you and familiarize yourself with their admission requirements and application processes.

6. Seek Apprenticeships or Vocational Programs: Not all career paths require a traditional four-year degree. Consider vocational programs or apprenticeships that provide hands-on training and skill development in specific industries. These programs can lead to rewarding careers and often have high job placement rates.

Remember, developing alternative plans does not mean giving up on your dream college or university. It simply means being proactive and prepared for different outcomes. By exploring alternative options, you may discover new pathways that lead to academic success and personal fulfillment. Stay positive and keep an open mind throughout this process.

Chapter 11
Preparing for College Life

Adjusting to independence and responsibility

Adjusting to independence and responsibility is a fundamental aspect of the college experience. As a high school student, you are accustomed to a structured environment with familiar routines and specific guidelines. In college, however, you will have newfound freedom and responsibilities.

One key adjustment is managing your time effectively. High school often provides a set schedule with classes and activities predetermined for you. In college, you will have more control over your schedule and must learn to balance academic commitments, extracurricular involvement, and personal responsibilities. Developing time management skills, such as creating a weekly schedule, setting priorities, and avoiding procrastination, will greatly contribute to your success.

Another aspect of independence in college is taking ownership of your education. Unlike high school, where teachers often guide and remind you about assignments and deadlines, college professors expect you to take initiative. This means attending classes regularly, actively participating in discussions, completing readings and assignments on time, and seeking help when needed. Embrace this opportunity to develop your self-discipline and self-motivation, which are crucial for academic achievement.

College life also introduces financial responsibility. As a college student, you may have access to credit cards, manage your own budget, and make financial decisions independently. It is important to develop good financial habits early on, such as budgeting, tracking expenses, and prioritizing needs over wants. Understanding the basics of personal finance, such as saving money and avoiding excessive debt, will set you on a path towards financial independence and stability.

Living away from home for the first time is another significant aspect of college life. Whether you choose to live on campus or off-campus, you will need to navigate the challenges of living independently. This includes managing household chores, cooking meals, and maintaining a healthy and balanced lifestyle. It is important to develop basic life skills, such as laundry, grocery shopping, and basic first aid, to ensure a smooth transition to independent living.

Lastly, adjusting socially is an essential part of the college experience. High school often revolves around a small community of familiar faces, but college introduces you to a diverse and larger student body. Embrace the opportunity to meet new people, engage in extracurricular activities, and join clubs or organizations that align with your interests. Building a social support network will not only enhance your college experience but also provide a sense of belonging and support.

In summary, adjusting to independence and responsibility in college entails effective time management, taking ownership of your education, developing good financial habits, acquiring basic life skills, and building a social network. Embrace these challenges as opportunities for personal growth and strive to make the most of your college experience.

Navigating Academic Challenges in College

College academics bring a new level of rigor and demand compared to high school. To succeed in this academically challenging environment, students need to develop effective study habits, manage their time wisely, and seek academic support when needed.

One crucial aspect of college academics is time management. Unlike high school, where students have a structured schedule, college offers more flexibility and freedom. This newfound independence can be both exciting and overwhelming. To effectively manage their time, students should create a schedule that includes not only their class times but also dedicated study blocks, extracurricular activities, and personal time. This will help them stay organized and prioritize their tasks.

In college, students must take ownership of their education. They should actively engage in their coursework, attend classes regularly, and participate in discussions. Professors expect students to come prepared, complete assignments on time, and actively participate in class activities. This level of engagement not only helps students gain a deeper understanding of the subject matter but also fosters a positive relationship with professors, which can be beneficial for seeking advice or future recommendations.

Academic support resources are readily available in colleges and universities. Students should take advantage of tutoring services, study groups, and office hours with professors. These resources can help clarify concepts, resolve doubts, and strengthen their understanding of the material. It is essential for students to proactively seek help when needed, as struggling in silence can lead to academic setbacks.

In addition to academic challenges, college life also requires students to adapt to a new social environment. Building a social network is crucial for emotional well-being and overall college experience. Students should actively participate in campus activities, join clubs or organizations that align with their interests, and connect with fellow students. These social interactions can lead to lifelong friendships, as well as opportunities for personal and professional growth.

In summary, navigating academic challenges in college requires students to develop effective study habits, manage their time wisely, take ownership of their education, seek academic support when needed, and build a social network. Embracing these challenges as opportunities for personal growth will not only help students succeed academically but also make the most of their college experience.

Social life and extracurriculars in college

As students prepare for college life, it is important to consider the social aspect of their new journey. College offers a unique opportunity to meet new people, explore different interests, and engage in a wide range of extracurricular activities. This chapter will provide guidance on navigating the social landscape of college and making the most of your social life while maintaining a healthy balance with academics.

One of the first things to keep in mind is that college is a diverse and inclusive environment. It is a chance to meet people from various backgrounds, cultures, and experiences. Embracing this diversity can enrich your college experience and broaden your perspective. Take the time to engage with your peers, participate in multicultural events, and join clubs or organizations that align with your interests. Doing so will help you build meaningful connections and foster a sense of belonging within the college community.

In addition to the academic workload, extracurricular activities play a vital role in college life. They provide opportunities to develop new skills, explore passions, and make lifelong friendships. Whether it's joining a sports team, becoming a member of a student organization, or participating in community service projects, extracurriculars can enhance personal growth and complement your academic journey.

When choosing extracurricular activities, consider your interests and goals. Look for opportunities that align with your passions and career aspirations. For example, if you have an interest in journalism, joining the college newspaper or a media club can provide valuable hands-on experience. Similarly, if you're interested in environmental issues, consider joining a sustainability group or volunteering for environmental initiatives on campus. By actively engaging in extracurriculars, you not only enhance your college experience but also demonstrate your commitment and involvement to future employers or graduate schools.

Finding a balance between academics and social life is crucial. While college offers numerous opportunities for socializing, it's important to prioritize your studies. Develop effective time management skills, establish a study schedule, and create a conducive learning environment. Set realistic goals and make sure to allocate time for both academic and social activities. Remember, college is an opportunity to grow academically and socially, and finding the right balance will contribute to your overall success and well-being.

Lastly, take advantage of the various resources and support systems available on campus. Universities often have counseling services, career centers, and mentorship programs that can offer guidance and support during your college journey. These resources can help you navigate through any challenges or transitions you may face, ensuring a smooth and fulfilling college experience.

In conclusion, college is not just about academics; it's a time to explore new friendships, interests, and experiences. Embrace the diverse community, engage in extracurricular activities that align with your passions, and find a balance between your social and academic commitments. By doing so, you will make the most of your college years and create memories that will last a lifetime.

Managing stress and maintaining well-being

Managing stress and maintaining well-being are essential aspects of college life. As students face the demands of academics, extracurricular activities, and social engagements, it becomes crucial to prioritize self-care and develop healthy coping mechanisms.

One effective strategy for managing stress is to establish a routine. Creating a structured schedule helps students stay organized and maximize their productivity. By allocating specific time slots for studying, attending classes, and engaging in recreational activities, students can maintain a healthy work-life balance. Additionally, incorporating self-care activities such as exercise, mindfulness, and relaxation techniques into their daily routine can help reduce stress levels and promote overall well-being.

Another important aspect of managing stress is seeking support from friends, family, and campus resources. Building a strong support network provides students with a sense of belonging and can greatly contribute to their mental health. It is important to reach out to trusted individuals when feeling overwhelmed or in need of guidance. College campuses often offer counseling services, peer support groups, and wellness programs, which can provide valuable resources and assistance.

Time management is also crucial in managing stress and maintaining well-being. Procrastination can lead to increased stress levels and a decreased sense of accomplishment. By practicing effective time management skills, such as setting realistic goals, breaking tasks into smaller, manageable chunks, and utilizing productivity techniques like the Pomodoro Technique, students can avoid unnecessary stress and achieve a greater sense of control over their workload.

Additionally, taking care of one's physical health plays a significant role in overall well-being. Proper nutrition, regular exercise, and sufficient sleep are essential for maintaining energy levels and managing stress. It is important for students to prioritize their health by making healthy food choices, engaging in regular physical activity, and ensuring they get an adequate amount of sleep each night.

In summary, managing stress and maintaining well-being are crucial for college students. By establishing a routine, seeking support, practicing effective time management, and prioritizing physical health, students can navigate the challenges of college life with resilience and come out with a fulfilling and successful college experience.

Chapter 12
Parents' Role in the College Process

Providing guidance and support

Parents play a crucial role in supporting and guiding their children through the college application process. As the process can be daunting and overwhelming for students, parents can provide valuable assistance to ensure their child's success.

One of the most important ways that parents can support their children is by offering guidance. This includes helping them research and explore potential colleges and universities. Parents can encourage their children to attend college fairs and visit campuses to get a better understanding of the different options available to them. By providing guidance and resources, parents can help their children make informed decisions about which institutions align with their academic and personal goals.

Financial support is another significant aspect of a parent's role in the college process. Parents can help their children navigate the complexities of financial aid, scholarships, and grants. They can assist in completing the Free Application for Federal Student Aid (FAFSA) and other required financial aid forms. By familiarizing themselves with the financial aid process, parents can help their children secure the necessary funds for their education.

Equally important is the emotional encouragement parents can provide throughout the college application journey. Applying to college can be emotionally charged, with students experiencing anxiety, stress, and self-doubt. Parents can offer a sense of reassurance and motivate their children to persevere. By being a source of emotional support, parents can help alleviate their child's worries and boost their confidence.

It is vital for parents to respect their child's independence during this process. While parents should offer guidance and support, it is essential to remember that the ultimate decision lies with the student. Encouraging their children to take charge of the college application process fosters independence and empowers them to take ownership of their future.

To actively participate in their child's college journey, parents should stay informed about important deadlines, requirements, and any changes in the application process. They can create a timeline together and establish a plan to ensure that all necessary steps are completed in a timely manner. By being proactive and engaged, parents can help their children stay organized and avoid any last-minute panics or oversights.

In conclusion, parents play a vital role in the college application process. By offering guidance, financial support, emotional encouragement, and respecting their child's independence, parents can assist their children in navigating the complex path to college. Collaborating with their children, parents can provide the necessary guidance and support, ultimately helping their child achieve their academic and personal goals.

Financial planning and support

Financial planning and support are essential aspects of parents' role in the college process. By offering guidance and assistance, parents can help their children navigate the often complex world of college finances and make informed decisions regarding their education.

One key aspect of financial planning is understanding the various costs associated with college. Parents can research and familiarize themselves with the expenses typically incurred, including tuition, fees, room and board, textbooks, and miscellaneous fees. This knowledge will enable them to have productive discussions with their children about the financial implications of their college choices.

Another important step is exploring financial aid options. Parents can support their children in researching and applying for scholarships, grants, and loans. They should ensure their child completes the Free Application for Federal Student Aid (FAFSA), as this is the gateway to federal financial aid programs. Additionally, parents can assist in seeking out local scholarships or other merit-based opportunities offered by organizations and institutions within their community.

It is crucial for parents to help their children understand the long-term financial implications of their college decisions. This includes discussing the possible need for student loans and explaining concepts such as interest rates, repayment terms, and loan forgiveness programs. Parents can also help their children create a budget to manage expenses during their college years.

Additionally, parents should explore college savings plans and options such as 529 plans to help fund their child's education. These plans offer tax advantages and can be an effective tool for setting money aside specifically for college expenses. Parents can seek guidance from financial advisors or explore online resources to determine the best savings strategy for their individual circumstances.

It is important to remember that financial support goes beyond just money. Parents can provide emotional support and encouragement during the college process, especially when financial concerns arise. By actively listening and offering guidance, parents can help alleviate some of the stress their children may feel about financing their education.

While parents play a crucial role in financial planning and support, it is also important for them to respect their child's independence in making financial decisions. Parents should foster an open and non-judgmental environment where their child feels comfortable discussing their financial concerns and aspirations. By empowering their children to take ownership of their financial choices, parents can prepare them for the financial responsibilities they will face in college and beyond.

Overall, parents' involvement in financial planning and support is vital during the college process. By offering guidance, researching financial aid options, and providing emotional encouragement, parents can contribute to their children's success in achieving their educational goals.

Emotional support and encouragement

In addition to providing financial support, parents also play a critical role in offering emotional support and encouragement to their children throughout the college application process. This chapter will explore various strategies parents can employ to create a positive and supportive environment for their children.

One of the most important aspects of emotional support is open communication. Encourage your child to express their fears, concerns, and aspirations about the college application process. Take the time to actively listen to their thoughts and validate their emotions. By fostering an environment of trust and understanding, you can alleviate some of their anxiety and help them feel supported.

It is essential to remind your child that their worth is not solely determined by whether they get into a specific college or university. Reinforce the idea that there are numerous paths to success and that their unique talents and abilities will shine no matter where they end up. By promoting a healthy perspective, you can help alleviate the pressure they may be feeling.

In addition to listening and offering reassurance, parents can also assist in the practical aspects of the college application process. Encourage your child to create a realistic timeline and set achievable goals. Help them research different colleges and universities, exploring their potential majors, extracurricular activities, and overall campus culture. Attend college fairs together and schedule campus visits to further engage with the decision-making process.

While it's important to be involved, it's equally vital to respect your child's independence. Give them space to make their own decisions and learn from any mistakes they may encounter. Offer guidance when needed, but ultimately let them take ownership of their college journey. This will empower them and foster a sense of responsibility.

Lastly, celebrate your child's achievements and milestones throughout the college application process. Whether it's submitting their applications, receiving acceptance letters, or even navigating rejections, acknowledge their hard work and resilience. By validating their efforts, you can boost their confidence and encourage them to continue striving for success.

Remember, the emotional support and encouragement you provide as a parent can greatly impact your child's overall well-being during this crucial time. By creating an open and supportive environment, you will enable them to navigate the college application process with more confidence and resilience.

Balancing Involvement and Independence

Finding the right balance between involvement and independence is crucial for parents navigating the college application process with their children. While providing support and guidance, it is important for parents to empower their children to take ownership of their own college journey.

One way to strike this balance is through open communication. Encourage your child to share their thoughts, concerns, and aspirations about their college plans. Actively listen to their ideas and validate their feelings, allowing them to express themselves freely. Avoid imposing your own expectations or desires upon them, as this can hinder their ability to make independent decisions.

Promote a healthy perspective by discussing the range of post-high school options available to your child. Help them understand that college is just one pathway to success and that there are various other avenues for personal and professional growth. By doing so, you help alleviate any undue pressure they may feel to follow a predetermined path.

Assisting with practical aspects of the college application process is another way to provide support. Offer guidance on navigating college websites, researching scholarships, and organizing important documents. Empower your child to take the lead in these tasks, but be available to provide assistance when needed.

Financial support is often a critical factor in college decisions. Begin by having an open and honest conversation about your family's financial situation. Together, explore options for financial aid, scholarships, or part-time employment. Emphasize the importance of planning and budgeting, helping them understand the long-term implications of their financial choices.

While involvement is necessary, it is equally crucial to respect your child's independence throughout this process. Avoid micromanaging their every move or making decisions on their behalf. Allow them to take ownership of researching potential colleges, scheduling campus visits, and reaching out to admissions offices. Nurture their ability to problem-solve and advocate for themselves.

As your child progresses through the application process, celebrate their achievements along the way. Recognize their hard work, dedication, and resilience. A positive and supportive environment will not only boost their confidence but also encourage them to persevere.

Remember, every student's college journey is unique. Be mindful of not projecting your own experiences or unfulfilled dreams onto your child. Stay objective and open-minded, valuing their individual choices and aspirations.

By finding the delicate balance between involvement and independence, parents can actively support their children throughout the college application process. This approach fosters personal growth, resilience, and the development of crucial life skills that extend far beyond the college years.

Chapter 13
Special Considerations

Applying as an international student

Applying as an international student brings a unique set of considerations and challenges to the college application process. For students who come from outside the United States, navigating the intricacies of the American higher education system can feel overwhelming. However, with proper guidance and preparation, international students can successfully navigate the application process and find their path to a good college or university.

One important factor for international students is understanding the different requirements and procedures for applying to colleges in the United States. It is essential to research and familiarize yourself with the specific admission criteria and deadlines of each institution you are interested in. Make sure you have a clear understanding of the standardized tests such as the SAT or ACT that may be required, as well as any additional tests specifically for international students like the TOEFL or IELTS.

Additionally, international students should pay close attention to the application process itself. A well-rounded application includes not only academic achievements but also extracurricular activities, leadership roles, and community involvement. It is crucial to highlight your unique experiences, cultural background, and any intercultural experiences that can contribute to the diversity of the campus community.

Another key consideration for international students is demonstrating English language proficiency. Many colleges and universities require English proficiency tests, such as the TOEFL or IELTS, to ensure that students have the necessary language skills to succeed academically. It is important to dedicate time and effort to improving your English language abilities, both written and spoken, to perform well on these tests.

One potential hurdle for international students is the financial aspect of studying in the United States. Tuition fees and living expenses can be substantial, and it is crucial to research and understand the available financial aid options for international students. Scholarships, grants, or work-study programs specifically designed for international students can help alleviate some of the financial burden.

Furthermore, international students should reach out to the international student services office at each college or university they are interested in. These offices provide valuable support and guidance throughout the application process and can help answer any questions or concerns you may have. They can also provide information on visa requirements, housing options, and cultural adjustment resources, ensuring a smooth transition to college life in the United States.

Being an international student brings unique perspectives and experiences to college campuses in the United States. By properly understanding and addressing the specific considerations and challenges faced by international students, you can successfully navigate the college application process and find the right educational opportunity that aligns with your academic and personal goals.

College Applications for Student-Athletes

Applying to college as a student-athlete comes with its own set of considerations and requirements. Balancing both academics and athletics can be challenging, but with proper planning and preparation, you can successfully navigate the college application process.

1. Academic Eligibility:

Before you can be recruited by college coaches, it is essential to meet the academic eligibility requirements set by both the NCAA (National Collegiate Athletic Association) and the specific college or university you are applying to. These requirements may involve maintaining a certain GPA, completing specific high school courses, and achieving a minimum standardized test score. Make sure to research and understand the academic eligibility criteria to ensure you are on track.

2. Communication with College Coaches:

If you are interested in playing sports at the college level, it is crucial to reach out and communicate with college coaches in your chosen sport. This can be done through email, phone calls, or attending recruitment events. Building a rapport with coaches can increase your chances of being recruited and provide valuable insights into the athletic programs of different colleges.

3. Highlighting Athletic Achievements:

When completing your college applications, be sure to include your athletic achievements and experiences. This can be done through your resume, personal statement, or supplemental essays. Describe your accomplishments, awards, and any leadership roles you have held within your sport. This information will help demonstrate your dedication, commitment, and potential to college admissions officers.

4. NCAA Eligibility Center:

For student-athletes aspiring to compete at the NCAA Division I or II level, it is essential to register with the NCAA Eligibility Center. This centralized organization verifies the academic and amateurism eligibility of prospective student-athletes. Registering with the NCAA Eligibility Center is a crucial step in the college application process for student-athletes.

5. Time Management:

As a student-athlete, effectively managing your time is vital. Balancing rigorous academic coursework, practice sessions, and competitions can be demanding. Develop good time management skills, create a schedule, and prioritize your commitments. This not only helps you stay on track academically but also demonstrates your ability to handle the demands of college life.

6. Letters of Recommendation:

Ask your coaches, athletic trainers, or teachers for letters of recommendation that emphasize your dedication, work ethic, and teamwork. These letters provide valuable insights into your character and can further support your application.

7. Be Realistic:

While pursuing your dreams as a student-athlete, it is essential to be realistic about your athletic abilities and potential scholarships. Research different colleges and universities that offer your desired sport and evaluate your chances of participating at different competition levels. Keep in mind that academics should also be a priority, as most student-athletes do not go on to play professionally.

By considering these factors and taking the necessary steps, you can successfully navigate the college application process as a student-athlete. Remember, your athletic pursuits should complement your academic goals, and finding the right balance will set you up for success in college and beyond.

Students with special needs and accommodations

Students with special needs and accommodations often face unique challenges when applying to college. However, with proper guidance and support, they can navigate the college application process successfully.

One important consideration for students with special needs is to understand their rights and the resources available to them. Under federal law, students with disabilities are protected by the Individuals with Disabilities Education Act (IDEA) and the Americans with Disabilities Act (ADA). These laws ensure that students have access to appropriate accommodations and support services throughout their education, including during the college application process.

To begin, students should make themselves aware of the accommodations and support services offered by the colleges they are interested in. This information can typically be found on the college's website or by contacting the disability services office directly. Understanding the type of accommodations available, such as extended testing time or note-taking assistance, can help students determine which colleges are the best fit for their needs.

In addition to researching accommodations, students should also consider reaching out to the disability services office at each college they are applying to. This can help establish a connection early on and allow students to ask any questions they may have about the application process. It is important for students to be proactive in advocating for themselves and clearly communicating their needs and requirements.

When filling out college applications, students should disclose their disability and any accommodations they have received in the past. While this may feel daunting, it is essential for colleges to understand the student's unique circumstances and educational history. This information can provide context for academic achievements and help colleges make informed decisions regarding admissions.

Furthermore, students should gather and organize documentation that verifies their disability and supports their request for accommodations. This may include medical records, diagnostic evaluations, or Individualized Education Programs (IEPs). The documentation should be recent and comprehensive, providing a clear picture of the student's needs and abilities.

Letters of recommendation can also play a crucial role in the college application process for students with special needs. It is important for students to choose recommenders who have worked closely with them and can speak to their abilities, strengths, and potential to succeed in a college setting. These letters can provide valuable insight into a student's character, determination, and ability to overcome challenges.

Lastly, students with special needs should be realistic about their college choices. It is essential to consider whether the colleges being considered have the appropriate resources and support systems available. Students should aim to find colleges that not only offer the desired academic programs but also have a strong commitment to inclusivity and accessibility.

In conclusion, students with special needs and accommodations can successfully navigate the college application process by understanding their rights, researching accommodations, establishing a connection with disability services offices, disclosing their disability, gathering necessary documentation, obtaining strong letters of recommendation, and being realistic about their college choices. With proper support and preparation, students with special needs can find the right college to help them succeed academically and personally.

Other unique scenarios and considerations

While the previous segment focused on students with special needs, there are other unique situations that high school students may find themselves in when navigating the college application process. In this section, we will explore how international students and student-athletes can approach the application process and provide tailored advice for these specific circumstances.

Applying as an international student:

For students who are from another country and seeking admission to colleges and universities in the United States, there are a few additional steps and considerations to keep in mind.

First and foremost, international students should research the specific requirements for international applicants at each institution they are interested in. While some colleges may require standardized test scores, such as the SAT or

ACT, others may have alternative criteria for evaluating international applicants.

It is also crucial for international students to demonstrate proficiency in English, as this will be necessary for success in their academic pursuits. Many colleges and universities require international students to submit scores from tests like the TOEFL (Test of English as a Foreign Language) or the IELTS (International English Language Testing System). It is important to prepare and take these tests well in advance of application deadlines.

Additionally, international students should consider the cost of attending college in the United States. Tuition and fees for international students are often higher than those for in-state or out-of-state students. Financial planning is essential in order to ensure that all expenses can be covered, including tuition, housing, healthcare, and living expenses. Scholarships and financial aid opportunities specifically available to international students should also be explored.

Navigating the college application process as a student-athlete:

For high school students who are also dedicated student-athletes, there are specific considerations that need to be taken into account when applying to colleges.

Student-athletes must balance their athletic commitments with their academic responsibilities. It is essential to maintain high academic performance while also devoting sufficient time and effort to their chosen sport. Student-athletes should communicate with their coaches and academic advisors to ensure they meet all eligibility requirements for college athletics.

In terms of the college application process, student-athletes should research colleges and universities that offer athletic programs in their chosen sport. They should reach out to coaches and athletic departments to express their interest and provide relevant athletic achievements and statistics.

It is important for student-athletes to emphasize their dedication, teamwork, leadership skills, and ability to manage time effectively in their application essays and throughout the application process. College coaches will be looking for athletes who not only excel in their chosen sport but also demonstrate qualities that align with their team's values and goals.

Student-athletes should be aware of the NCAA (National Collegiate Athletic Association) eligibility rules and regulations, as well as any specific guidelines set by their sport's governing body. These rules may impact the recruitment process and eligibility for athletic scholarships.

By understanding and addressing the unique circumstances and considerations surrounding international students and student-athletes, high school students can effectively navigate the college application process. With careful planning, research, and communication, they can maximize their chances of finding the right college or university that suits their individual needs and aspirations.

Chapter 14
Life After Acceptance

Deciding on the final college choice

After months of hard work and anticipation, you've finally received acceptance letters from multiple colleges. Congratulations! This chapter will guide you through the crucial process of deciding on the final college choice. While it may feel overwhelming to make such an important decision, remember that you have already accomplished a great deal in getting to this point.

To begin, it's important to reflect on your goals and priorities. Consider what you hope to achieve academically, socially, and personally during your college years. Think about the specific programs, majors, and extracurricular activities that each institution offers. Take into account the location, campus culture, and the overall environment. As you evaluate your options, make a list of pros and cons to help you weigh the factors that matter most to you.

Next, you should conduct thorough research on each college you are considering. Utilize reliable resources such as college websites, guidebooks, and online forums to gather information about the academic reputation, faculty, and support services available at each institution. Look for reviews or testimonials from current or former students, as they can provide valuable insights into the college experience.

While researching, pay attention to specific factors that pertain to your individual circumstances. If you have a particular academic or career interest, explore whether the college offers specialized programs or research opportunities in that field. If you have any special needs or accommodations, ensure that the college can provide the necessary support.

It is also important to consider the financial aspect of your decision. Evaluate the financial aid packages offered by each college, including scholarships, grants, and loans. Compare the total cost of attendance, factoring in tuition, fees, room and board, and other expenses. Be realistic about what you and your family can afford and carefully consider the potential long-term impact of student loan debt.

Once you have gathered all the necessary information, it is helpful to visit the campuses in person, if possible. Attend campus tours, sit in on classes, and talk to current students and faculty. This firsthand experience will give you a better sense of the campus community and whether it aligns with your expectations and goals.

Finally, consult with your parents, mentors, and trusted advisors. Seek their perspective and guidance as they can offer valuable insights and help you see the decision from different angles. Discuss your options openly, but remember that the ultimate decision should be yours alone.

Remember, the college you choose will be your home for the next four years or more. Take your time with this decision and trust your instincts. As you evaluate your options, remain confident that the hard work you have put into your high school years has prepared you to make the best choice for your future. Good luck on this exciting journey of selecting your final college choice!

Preparing for the Transition to College

Once you have made the final decision on which college to attend, it's time to start preparing for the exciting journey ahead. The transition from high school to college can be both thrilling and overwhelming, but with the right strategies and preparations, you can set yourself up for success. This section of the book will guide you through the essential steps to help ease your transition and ensure a smooth start to your college experience.

1. Familiarize Yourself with Campus Resources

College campuses are filled with a wide range of resources and support services aimed at helping students thrive academically, socially, and emotionally. Take the time to familiarize yourself with these resources before you start classes. Visit the college website or reach out to the admissions office to gather information about tutoring centers, academic advising, counseling services, career development centers, and student organizations. Understanding what is available to you will enable you to make the most of your college experience.

2. Develop Time Management Skills

College life often comes with increased responsibilities and demands on your time. It's important to develop effective time management skills to stay on top of your coursework, extracurricular activities, and personal commitments. Consider creating a schedule or using a planner to help prioritize tasks and allocate your time effectively. Learning to balance your academic and social life early on will help you avoid unnecessary stress and ensure that you make the most of your college experience.

3. Learn about Course Registration and Curricular Requirements

Understanding the process of course registration and the curricular requirements of your chosen major is crucial. Familiarize yourself with the college's course catalog and academic policies to ensure you are on track to meet your educational goals. Some colleges may have specific prerequisites or recommended courses for incoming students. Planning your class schedule in advance and consulting with academic advisors will help you stay organized and ensure a smooth transition to college academics.

4. Cultivate Healthy Study Habits

College coursework often requires more independent studying and self-discipline compared to high school. It's essential to cultivate healthy study habits to excel academically. Find a study environment that works best for you, whether it's the library, a coffee shop, or your dorm room. Experiment with different study techniques such as creating study guides, participating in study groups, or using online resources. Developing effective study habits early on will set you up for success throughout your college journey.

5. Prepare for a New Social Environment

College provides an opportunity to meet new people from diverse backgrounds and cultures. Embrace the chance to expand your social network and make new friends. Attend orientation events, join clubs and organizations that align with your interests, and participate in campus activities. However, also remember to strike a balance between socializing and maintaining a focus on your academic responsibilities.

6. Take Care of Your Physical and Mental Health

College life can be demanding, so it's crucial to prioritize your physical and mental well-being. Make sure to maintain a healthy lifestyle by eating nutritious meals, getting regular exercise, and getting enough sleep. Additionally, be aware of the support services available on campus for mental health concerns. Reach out to counselors or support groups if you're feeling overwhelmed or struggling with the transition.

By following these steps and incorporating them into your pre-college preparations, you'll set yourself up for a successful transition to college life. Remember that each college experience is unique, and it's crucial to stay open-minded, adaptable, and proactive in making the most of your time at college.

Setting goals for college success

Setting goals for college success is crucial for ensuring a fulfilling and productive academic journey. As you embark on this new chapter of your life, it's essential to have a clear vision of what you want to achieve and the steps you need to take to reach your goals. In this section, we will explore the importance of goal setting and provide practical strategies to help you set and achieve your objectives.

Why Set Goals?

Setting goals provides you with a sense of direction and purpose. By defining what you want to accomplish during your college years, you can prioritize your efforts and stay motivated throughout your academic journey. Goals give you something to strive for and serve as a roadmap to success.

Types of Goals

There are various types of goals you can set for yourself in college. Here are a few examples:

1. Academic Goals: These relate to your academic performance and achievements. Do you want to maintain a certain GPA, make the Dean's List, or earn a specific scholarship? Setting academic goals can help you stay focused and dedicated to your studies.

2. Career Goals: What do you hope to achieve professionally after graduation? Do you have a specific career path in mind? Setting career goals can guide your choice of major, internships, and extracurricular activities,

ensuring you acquire the necessary skills and experiences for your desired profession.

3. Personal Development Goals: College is an excellent opportunity for personal growth and self-discovery. Setting personal development goals can include improving your public speaking skills, cultivating effective leadership abilities, or enhancing your critical thinking capabilities.

4. Social and Extracurricular Goals: College is also about making connections and building a well-rounded experience. Setting goals related to your social life and involvement in clubs, organizations, or sports can help you develop valuable networking skills and create lasting memories.

Strategies for Goal Setting

To effectively set and achieve your goals, consider the following strategies:

1. Be Specific: Clearly define your goals, making them measurable and concrete. Avoid vague statements such as "do well in college" and instead set specific targets like "achieve a 3.5 GPA in my first semester."

2. Break Goals Down: Divide larger goals into smaller, manageable tasks. This approach allows you to track your progress and celebrate milestones along the way.

3. Set Deadlines: Assign deadlines to your goals and tasks. This promotes accountability and helps you stay on track.

4. Prioritize: Determine which goals are most important to you and focus your time and energy accordingly. Prioritization ensures that you allocate resources effectively.

5. Write Them Down: Document your goals in a physical or digital format. Writing them down solidifies your commitment and serves as a constant reminder of what you're working towards.

6. Seek Support: Don't be afraid to share your goals with friends, family, or mentors. They can offer encouragement, guidance, and hold you accountable.

Remember, setting goals isn't enough – it's essential to create actionable plans and take the necessary steps to achieve them. Embrace the challenges and opportunities that college presents, and use your goals to guide you on your path to success.

Summer activities before college

Summer activities before college can be a great way for students to make the most of their remaining free time and prepare for the exciting journey ahead. While it's essential to take a break and recharge, it's also wise to use the summer as an opportunity to engage in valuable activities that will help set you up for success in college.

One option to consider is finding a part-time job or internship related to your intended field of study. This will not only provide you with real-world experience but also allow you to start building your professional network. Many employers offer summer programs specifically designed for high school students, so it's worth exploring these opportunities.

Another activity that can be beneficial is volunteering. Look for local organizations or community service programs that align with your interests. Not only will this contribute to your personal growth, but it will also demonstrate your commitment to making a positive impact. Plus, volunteering can help you develop important skills such as teamwork, leadership, and empathy.

If you're interested in expanding your knowledge and exploring new subjects, consider taking online courses or attending summer programs at universities. Many colleges offer pre-college programs that allow high school students to experience campus life and get a taste of college-level courses. These programs can help you discover new passions or deepen existing ones, all while getting a head start on earning college credits.

In addition to academic and professional pursuits, it's crucial to prioritize your mental and physical well-being. Use the summer as an opportunity to establish healthy habits such as regular exercise, proper sleep, and a balanced diet. Engage in activities that bring you joy and help reduce stress, such as spending time with friends and family, practicing mindfulness, or pursuing hobbies.

Lastly, don't forget to take care of practical matters before heading off to college. Make sure you have all the necessary documents, such as your student ID, health insurance information, and any required immunization records. Take the time to review your financial aid package and understand your tuition payment options. If you plan to live on-campus, familiarize yourself with what you're allowed to bring and what is provided. These small but essential tasks will ensure a smooth transition into college life.

Remember, the goal of summer activities before college is to balance relaxation and preparation. Take the time to unwind and enjoy your last summer as a high school student, but also seize the opportunity to engage in activities that will benefit your future. By making intentional choices and setting yourself up for success, you'll be ready to make the most of your college experience from day one.

Chapter 15
Index

As the concluding chapter, this section serves as a comprehensive index, providing quick access to various topics, resources, and references mentioned throughout the book. It will be a valuable tool for readers to easily find information.

Topic-Wise Index:

1. Introduction to College Applications

   - Understanding the college application process

   - Exploring different types of colleges and universities

2. Academic Preparation

   - Choosing the right courses in high school

- Preparing for standardized tests (SAT, ACT)

- Maintaining a strong GPA

- Seeking academic support and resources

3. Extracurricular Activities and Leadership

- Exploring different extracurricular options

- Building a well-rounded resume

- Developing leadership skills

- Participating in community service and volunteer work

4. Researching Colleges and Universities

- Factors to consider when choosing a college

- Using college search tools and websites

- Visit and explore college campuses

- Connecting with current college students

5. Financial Planning for College

- Understanding the cost of college

- Scholarships, grants, and financial aid options

- Creating a budget and saving for college expenses

- Considering student loans and repayment options

6. Writing College Essays and Personal Statements

   - Understanding the essay prompts

   - Brainstorming and planning your essay

   - Writing a compelling personal statement

   - Editing and revising your essay

7. Letters of Recommendation and Interviews

   - Selecting the right recommenders

   - Preparing for college interviews

   - Presenting yourself confidently

   - Following up after interviews

8. Application Submission and Timeline

   - Deadlines for early decision, regular decision, and rolling admissions

   - Gathering required documents and information

   - Completing the Common Application or college-specific applications

   - Submitting applications and tracking their status

9. Understanding College Admissions Decisions

   - Different types of admissions decisions (acceptance, rejection, waitlist)

- Reviewing financial aid packages and scholarships

- Making a final college choice

- Understanding the enrollment process

10. Transitioning to College

- Preparing for the transition from high school to college

- Orientation programs and resources

- Packing essentials for college

- Navigating your first year on campus

This index provides a comprehensive overview of the topics covered in this guidebook. It serves as a quick reference tool for students and parents to easily find information and resources to help them navigate the college admissions process successfully. Use this index to locate specific chapters or sections that address your particular interests or concerns.

The Resources and References Index is a valuable section that provides an organized list of various resources and references mentioned throughout the book. It is designed to help readers easily locate specific information and dive deeper into the topics discussed. By utilizing this index, students and parents can access additional materials and explore further insights to enhance their understanding of the college admissions process.

Here are some notable resources and references included in the index:

1. Recommended Books:

   - "The College Admissions Mystique" by Bill Mayher

   - "The Fiske Guide to Colleges" by Edward Fiske

   - "The College Solution: A Guide for Everyone Looking for the Right School at the Right Price" by Lynn O'Shaughnessy

2. Online Research Tools:

   - College Board (collegeboard.org)

   - Naviance (naviance.com)

   - BigFuture by The College Board (bigfuture.collegeboard.org)

3. Academic Preparation:

   - Advanced Placement (AP) Courses

   - International Baccalaureate (IB) Program

   - SAT Subject Tests

4. Extracurricular Activities and Leadership:

   - Volunteer Opportunities

   - Sports Teams and Clubs

- Student Government and Leadership Roles

5. Financial Aid and Scholarships:

   - Free Application for Federal Student Aid (FAFSA)

   - CSS Profile

   - Scholarships.com

6. College Essay Writing:

   - Common Application Essay Prompts

   - Tips for Crafting a Compelling Essay

   - Editing and Proofreading Techniques

7. Letters of Recommendation and Interviews:

   - Selecting Appropriate Recommenders

   - Preparing for College Interviews

   - Common Interview Questions

8. Application Submission and Timeline:

   - Early Action, Early Decision, and Regular Decision

   - Application Deadlines

   - Application Components Checklist

9. Understanding College Admissions Decisions:

   - Acceptance, Waitlist, and Rejection Letters

- Deciphering Financial Aid and Merit Aid Offers

- Decision Appeals and Deferrals

10. Transitioning to College:

- Freshman Orientation and Housing

- Academic Advising and Course Selection

- Adjusting to College Life

This index serves as a valuable tool for students and parents to conveniently access the various resources and references mentioned in the book. By using this index, readers can explore further information and resources that supplement the content and aid them in their college admissions journey.

Quick Tips and Advice

The Quick Tips and Advice Index is a compilation of helpful suggestions and recommendations mentioned throughout this guide. It serves as a convenient reference for high school students and their parents, enabling them to quickly access key information and actionable steps to enhance their college preparation.

1. Academic Preparation

- Course Selection: Choosing a rigorous curriculum that aligns with college admissions requirements and reflects your academic strengths and interests.

- GPA and Class Rank: Understanding the importance of maintaining a competitive GPA and how it factors into college admissions decisions.

- Standardized Tests: Preparing for and taking the SAT or ACT, including tips for effective studying and test-taking strategies.

- Study Habits: Developing effective study habits to ensure academic success in high school and beyond.

2. Extracurricular Activities

- Identifying Passions: Exploring interests and finding meaningful extracurricular activities that align with your personal goals and values.

- Leadership Development: Taking on leadership roles within clubs, organizations, or community initiatives to demonstrate initiative and responsibility.

- Community Service: Participating in community service to contribute to society and showcase your commitment to making a positive impact.

- Sports and Athletics: Balancing athletic commitments with academic responsibilities, and leveraging sports achievements as part of your college application.

3. College Essay Writing

- Choosing a Topic: Selecting a compelling topic that showcases your unique experiences, values, and perspectives.

- Structure and Format: Organizing your thoughts and ideas in a clear and coherent manner, following the proper essay structure.

- Grammar and Style: Paying attention to grammar, syntax, and style to ensure your essay is polished and error-free.

- Seeking Feedback: Utilizing peer review or seeking guidance from teachers, counselors, or mentors to improve your essay.

4. Letters of Recommendation and Interviews

- Selecting Recommenders: Choosing individuals who can provide insightful and positive evaluations of your character, academic abilities, or achievements.

- Interview Preparation: Preparing for college interviews by researching common questions, practicing responses, and conducting mock interviews.

- Dressing and Presenting Yourself: Understanding appropriate attire and presenting yourself confidently and professionally during interviews.

5. Application Submission and College Admissions Decisions

- Meeting Deadlines: Keeping track of application deadlines and submitting all required materials by the specified dates.

- Application Components: Understanding the various components of a college application, such as the personal statement, letters of recommendation, and extracurricular involvement.

- College Admissions Decisions: Gaining insights into the different types of admissions decisions, including early action, early decision, regular decision, and deferred admissions.

6. Transitioning to College

- Academic Expectations: Familiarizing yourself with the academic expectations and rigor of college coursework.

- Social and Emotional Adjustment: Preparing for the social and emotional changes that come with transitioning to college life.

- Time Management: Developing effective time management skills to balance academic responsibilities, extracurricular activities, and personal obligations.

- Seeking Support: Identifying campus resources and seeking support from advisors, professors, or counseling services when needed.

Journey to success

As we reach the conclusion of this guide, it's important to reflect on the journey that lies ahead for students and parents navigating the path to college. The process, often daunting and complex, is also a journey of growth, discovery, and opportunity. This book has aimed to be more than just a guide; it's a companion on this transformative journey.

For students, the steps you take today lay the groundwork for your future. The college application process is not just about securing a place in a college; it's about understanding yourself, your goals, and your aspirations. It's about building a foundation for a lifetime of learning, growth, and success. Remember, the choices you make should align with your values, interests, and passions. College is a significant step, but it's also the beginning of a broader adventure in life.

Parents, your role in this journey is pivotal. Your support, guidance, and encouragement are invaluable assets to your child. However, it's also a time for you to trust in the lessons you've taught them, allowing them to take the lead in their journey. This process is as much about their growth as it is about your adaptation to their growing independence.

Throughout this guide, we've covered a myriad of topics—from understanding college options and preparing academically to financial planning and dealing with acceptances and rejections. Each chapter was designed to not only provide practical advice and information but also to empower you to make informed decisions with confidence and clarity.

As you close this book, remember that the path to college is unique for each student and family. Embrace this journey with an open mind, a willingness to learn, and the resilience to overcome challenges. The road to college may have its twists and turns, but the destination is worth every step.

Here's to the beginning of an exciting new chapter in your lives. May your journey to college be enriching, enlightening, and full of success.

Solomon Sahle